THE TAKER

TWO ORIGINAL CREEPSHOW™ NOVELS

THE TAKER

BY ELLEY COOPER

Scholastic Inc.

All rights reserved. Published by Scholastic Inc., *Publishers since 1920*. SCHOLASTIC and associated logos are trademarks and/or registered trademarks of Scholastic Inc.

The publisher does not have any control over and does not assume any responsibility for author or third-party websites or their content.

No part of this publication may be reproduced, stored in a retrieval system, or transmitted in any form or by any means, electronic, mechanical, photocopying, recording, or otherwise, without written permission of the publisher. For information regarding permission, write to Scholastic Inc., Attention: Permissions Department, 557 Broadway, New York, NY 10012.

This book is a work of fiction. Names, characters, places, and incidents are either the product of the author's imagination or are used fictitiously, and any resemblance to actual persons, living or dead, business establishments, events, or locales is entirely coincidental.

ISBN 978-1-338-63123-4

1 2020
Printed in the U.S.A.   23

First printing 2020

Book design by Jessica Meltzer
Comic art by Brent Schoonover
Photos © Shutterstock.

For my parents, who are cool for many reasons,
one of which is that they always let me
read spooky stuff.
—E.C.

TABLE OF CONTENTS

CHAPTER 1

I guess we shouldn't throw stones," Bea said as they pulled up in front of the new house.

"What?" her mom said, sounding distracted. She had been driving the moving van while Bea's dad and little brother, Charlie, followed behind in the car. They had hit the road at 6 a.m., and now it was almost dinnertime.

"There's that expression," Bea said, "that people who live in glass houses shouldn't throw stones. We shouldn't throw stones because this house has a *lot* of glass."

Mom smiled a little. "That's true. I like it, though. All the windows make everything feel so open and sunny."

In Bea's opinion, the new house was weird. The wood was unpainted, the windows were floor-to-ceiling, and there were lots of weird angles between the roof and walls. Her dad, who loved the new house, said it was an example of "postmodern architecture," whatever that meant. He thought the new house said a lot more about who they were as people than their old ranch-style house, which was "like living in a shoebox."

Bea already missed the nice, normal shoebox house in the neighborhood where she could walk to her best friend's house. She missed her old school and the dance studio where she had spent so much time that it felt like a second home.

Now no place felt like home.

She understood that they'd had no choice but to move. Her dad got laid off from his job, and her mom's part-time work didn't pay enough to support the family. New jobs in a new town had been the only option, but that didn't make it any easier. Especially since Bea was going to have to walk into school on her first day of eighth grade not knowing a single person.

"Isn't it great?" Dad stood outside the moving van with a huge grin on his face. He was wearing one of the bright-colored Hawaiian shirts he favored, and his long goatee had been twisted into a braid, of all things. "I can't believe we got such a great deal on this place! It's got charm to burn." He looked over at the house like a proud papa looking at his newborn baby. "It's so retro! Nothing looks more retro than something that was built to look ultramodern decades ago."

Mom smiled back at him. "Yeah, after we get unpacked we're going to have to hit the flea markets and find some kitschy '80s stuff like our parents had when we were kids. It'll look perfect in the house." Bea's mom was just as quirky as Bea's dad. She was partial to weird-colored nail polish and earrings made of random objects like guitar picks. She had even dyed a blue streak in her hair.

Sometimes Bea felt the urge to tell her parents to grow up.

"Oh, it won't look perfect," Dad said, offering Mom his arm as she stepped out of the van. "It'll look *radical*. Or tubular." He looked over at Bea. "That's '80s slang."

Bea breathed a heavy sigh. "I know it is. I'm not an idiot." She stepped out of the moving van onto the sidewalk.

"Nobody said you were," Mom said. "Don't be so touchy."

Bea didn't feel like she was being touchy. It was

just that her family was so annoying. Charlie was already in the front yard, running around, hitting a tree with a stick, and generally calling attention to his weirdness. She hoped none of the neighbors could see him. This wasn't the first impression she wanted to make.

"I guess the first thing we should do is get Devo into the house," Mom said.

"I'll do it," Bea volunteered. Devo was the family's tabby cat, named after some '80s band her parents liked, and he and Bea had a special bond. "I'm going to put him in my room first, okay?"

"Okay," Mom said. "But close the door so he doesn't get out while we're moving stuff in."

Bea picked up the cat carrier, and her mom opened the house's front door. The empty rooms in the house looked huge, cavernous. But the comparison to a cave stopped there because the sunlight pouring through the gigantic windows was blindingly bright. "Well, Devo, this is your new home. Your big, weird, new home," Bea said. She took the cat carrier up a staircase that looked like it belonged outside a kid's tree house instead of inside a real house. The first room on the right was the one she'd picked. It was smaller than her parents' room but bigger than Charlie's.

The air that was released when she opened the

door was at least twenty degrees colder than the air in the hall. Shouldn't rooms that had been shut up be hotter than the rest of the house? *One more weird thing about this place*, Bea thought. The house already looked weird enough with all its big windows and strange angles. Did its temperature have to be weird, too?

She set the cat carrier on the floor of her empty room and unlatched its door. "Welcome home, buddy," she said. When Devo didn't emerge, she squatted down to make sure he was okay. The vet had prescribed him a kitty tranquilizer for the trip, and when Bea peeked in at him, he opened one green eye, then closed it, and went back to sleep. "Okay, night-night, then," Bea said. As she stood to leave, a smell hit her nose, fruity and artificial. After a few sniffs, she identified it as grape bubble gum. But except for Devo in his carrier, the room was completely empty. Where could the smell be coming from?

Back outside, Dad was trying to organize the troops. "Okay," he said. "We just heard from the heavy-lifting guys. They should be here in about fifteen minutes. In the meantime, you kids grab the boxes with your names on them, and your mom and I will start unloading kitchen stuff."

⊰•◦⊱

By six o'clock, most of the stuff was in the house. Bea's room had her bed and dresser, and she had managed to set up Devo's food and water station and litter box. He had finally emerged from his cat carrier and was sniffing around suspiciously, sometimes emitting a low growl while staring at nothing. "Lots of new smells, huh, buddy?" Bea said. "If you figure out where that bubble-gum smell is coming from, let me know."

Bea heard footsteps and looked up to see Charlie standing in the door, his sandy-blond hair sticking up in random places like always. One of his shoes was untied. "Can you come help me with something for a minute?" he asked.

"Reluctantly," Bea said. She was busy unpacking the stuff she kept on her dresser—her jewelry box, her trophies from dance competitions, her favorite dance recital photos.

"Hey, your room's a lot colder than mine," Charlie said.

"Yeah, it must be the AC vent in here," Bea said, setting a figurine of a long-necked black cat on her dresser.

"The AC's not running," Charlie said. "Say, can I have a piece of your gum?"

"I don't have any gum," Bea said. She had given up

gum two years ago after some kid in class told her she chewed like a cow.

"I smell gum, though." Charlie sniffed the air. "That really soft grape kind."

Bea smelled it, too, as clearly as if it were in her own mouth, but she would rather give Charlie a hard time than agree with him. "I don't know what you're talking about," she said. "You must be hallucinating."

"You don't smell it?"

"Nope," Bea said, though the fake grapey aroma filled her nostrils.

"Bea! Charlie! Dinner!" Mom called from downstairs.

"How can there be dinner when the kitchen stuff isn't even unpacked yet?" Bea said.

"Maybe they got pizza—or burgers!" Charlie said with a hopeful look on his face.

Bea shook her head. "Do you really think we could be that lucky?" Their parents called fast-food restaurants "purveyors of poison," and the food they cooked at home tended to be absurdly healthy. Ratatouille. Stir-fried veggies with steamed brown rice. Scrambled tofu.

"No, probably not," Charlie said.

At the dining room table, they sat down to a loaf of bread, a jar of peanut butter, a jar of strawberry jam, and a pitcher of tap water. "Our first meal in our new home," Mom said, pouring water into paper cups. "Nothing fancy, but we'll do better when we know where the pots and pans are."

"And where a grocery store is," Dad added.

Bea thought PB&J was perfect. She already felt overwhelmed by her strange and new surroundings, and she was even more overwhelmed when she thought of starting at her new school on Monday. Right now, the taste of peanut butter and jelly felt like the only thing that was familiar.

CHAPTER 2

Bea stood in front of the mirror at her dresser. She didn't feel like she looked great, but she hoped she at least looked good enough for her first day of school. Good enough not to stand out as trying too hard or not trying hard enough. Middle-school girls were brutal, and it didn't help that she was doomed to be the New Kid.

After changing clothes three times, Bea had settled on skinny jeans and a light blue top that matched her light blue canvas slip-on shoes. If she were being honest with herself, she would admit that her sandy-blond hair was just as prone to sticking out in random places as her brother's, so she had brushed it back and secured it into a ponytail. Her parents wouldn't let her wear much in the way of makeup yet, which was too bad because she'd love to make her eyes all smoky like the girls she watched doing makeup tutorials online. At least she was allowed to use some mascara and lip gloss, provided she was the one who bought it. She had gotten her ears pierced for her thirteenth birthday, and tiny silver studs sparkled in her earlobes.

Good enough, she decided with a sigh. Because really, what choice did she have?

"You look adorable!" Mom said when Bea came into the kitchen.

Bea cringed. "Ew. 'Adorable' makes me sound like a tiny fuzzy kitten or something."

"Well, to me you're even more adorable than a tiny fuzzy kitten," Mom said. "Sit down and pour yourself some orange juice. The muffins are about to come out of the oven."

Bea knew from the fruity, cinnamony aroma that Mom had made her whole-grain apple-walnut muffins. They weren't bad, but they were dense, only lightly sweetened with agave, and unmistakably healthy. Bea wished she could have blueberry muffins made with white flour and sugar, the kind that were basically cake.

Charlie stumbled into the kitchen looking sleepy and disheveled and took his place at the table. "Are you guys excited about your first day?" Mom asked, setting down a saucer with a muffin in front of each of them.

"Nervous," Bea said, surprised to hear herself blurting out her true feelings.

"Why are you nervous?" Charlie asked, sounding genuinely puzzled.

"You'll understand when you're older." Bea knew it was the most maddening thing an older sister could say, but he had it coming for being so annoyingly calm all the time.

It was infuriating, really, how relaxed Charlie was about the move, about starting school, about everything. But he was still in elementary school, and elementary school was different than middle school. Plus, he was a boy. Boys could make friends in any setting. It was like taking a dog to a dog park to meet other dogs. You put them outside together, and they'd naturally start playing. Girls were different. They were more like cats. They had to size each other up before deciding if they were going to purr or hiss.

"Before you guys head out the door, I have to take your picture," Mom said, brandishing her phone.

"Mom, it's not the first day of kindergarten," Bea said. Sometimes it felt like Mom tried to annoy her on purpose.

"No, but it's your first day of eighth grade and Charlie's first day of fifth. This day will never come again, so scooch together and smile!"

When Mom showed them the picture, Charlie was smiling good-naturedly and Bea looked like she was being poked with a sharp stick.

⊰○○⊱

From the outside, the one-story red brick building that was Grant Middle School didn't look that different from Bea's old school. The physical similarity made the fact that the inside of the school was filled with unfamiliar faces even more disorienting.

Bea found her way to homeroom, then to English, then to math, moving when she heard the bell ring like she was some kind of programmed robot. All around her, people clearly knew each other and were already in their predetermined groups: the academic overachievers who obsessed over every word that came out of the teachers' mouths, the athletes who talked about sports all the time, the gamers who could only talk about what they were going to play as soon as they got home. Bea didn't see a group she could be a member of . . . or even one she would want to be a member of.

At lunchtime, she stood at the entrance of the

packed cafeteria. The din of all the kids who knew each other talking and laughing was too much. She couldn't face it. She ate the apple from the lunch her mom had packed as she walked down the hall, trying to look casual, as if she couldn't be bothered to take time out of her busy, fabulous life for something as mundane as lunch in the cafeteria. She stopped to study a bulletin board labeled *Clubs and Activities*. Of all the notices for band and 4-H and Chess Club, only one caught her eye: *Dance Team Tryouts*.

Bea had started taking dance lessons when she was six, not because her parents pushed her to, like so many of the other kids' parents had, but because she wanted to. Back home, she had spent every available hour in the dance studio, taking ballet, jazz, and tap. Ms. Lisa, her teacher at the studio was like a second mother to her, and some of the other girls in the classes, especially her BFFs, Lucy and Madison, were like her sisters. Bea couldn't think of how far she was from Lucy and Madison without her heart hurting.

When Bea was dancing, all her self-consciousness, all her worries, disappeared. The music filled her ears, and then it filled her body. She moved without thought or care, flowing as naturally as water. If there was one thing Bea knew about herself, it was that she could dance.

Tryouts were Wednesday, after school in the gym. She would be there.

Bea sat through science, then social studies, feeling increasingly invisible as friends whispered to each other around her. In the hall, as she was putting her social studies book in her locker, a voice said, "Hi."

She turned around to see a boy, shorter than she was, wearing glasses and a T-shirt with video game characters on it. He wasn't the sort of person she'd usually gravitate toward, but he was also the first non-teacher who'd spoken to her all day.

"Hi," she said.

"You're new." He smiled, showing a mouthful of braces.

"I know," she said.

He laughed. "I guess you do. I'm Ed."

"Bea."

Bea's attention was diverted by a band of girls walking down the hall. The one in the middle was tall and leggy, wearing a peach-colored sleeveless dress that was shorter than Bea's mom would let her get away with. Her features were soft and accented by delicate makeup, and her long, light blonde hair was luminous, as if touched by moonlight. The girl to her right wore leggings and a tank top that showed off her toned arms and legs. Her light brown skin had a warm glow, and her black hair was a dark cloud framing her flawless face. The third girl wore skinny jeans with wedge-heeled sandals and a white ruffled blouse. Her chestnut hair was a thick, shiny curtain.

Conversations stopped as these girls walked by. They seemed to leave a trail of glitter in their path. They were so glamorous and seemed so much older than the other middle schoolers around them. It was all Bea could do not to stand there with her mouth hanging open.

"Ed," Bea said. "Who are those girls?"

"Oh, them?" Ed said, giving the girls a sidelong glance. "They're on the dance team."

CHAPTER 3

Bea looked through her jewelry box again. They were gone.

It made no sense. Over the weekend, when she had unpacked the stuff for her room, she had found her jewelry box, which was sealed with packing tape for the move. She had taken off the tape and opened the box. Her jewelry had gotten jostled around on the ride in the moving van, but it was all accounted for: There was her silver chain with the birthstone pendant and the two pairs of earrings she had gotten for her birthday—small silver hoops from her parents and seed pearls from her grandma. So what had happened?

Bea went downstairs to the living room. Her mom

was sitting on the couch reading a novel, with Devo curled into a stripy ball on her lap.

"Mom, have you seen the seed pearl earrings Grandma gave me?"

Mom looked up from her book. "No. I hope they didn't get lost during the move."

"I know they didn't," Bea said. "That's what's weird. They were in my jewelry box the other night."

"Huh," her mom said. "That is weird. Well, maybe you just mislaid them, and they'll turn up." She looked back down at her book.

"But I wanted them for tomorrow," Bea said, feeling more upset than she'd known she was. Shouldn't her mom at least offer to help her look? "Dance team tryouts are tomorrow, and I wanted to wear them for good luck." The truth was, the pearl earrings were the most expensive jewelry Bea owned, and she had hoped they would make a good impression on the dance team girls.

"You don't need luck, kid," her mom said. "You've got talent."

Bea rolled her eyes and headed back upstairs. Clearly, her mom was going to be no help.

Bea checked her jewelry box again just to make sure she wasn't imagining things. The earrings were still gone.

"Hey, Bea."

Bea turned to see that Charlie, wearing his pajamas, had just walked right into her room. "Ever heard of knocking?"

"The door was open."

"Still."

"Okay," Charlie said, and knocked on the doorframe. "I can't find some of my trading cards. You haven't seen any lying around anywhere, have you?"

Charlie collected trading cards for some silly game he and other boys his age liked to play. It was a waste of money as far as Bea was concerned. "Why would I know where your stupid trading cards are?"

"I don't know. It's just that I know where I left them, and they weren't there."

Bea looked down at the jewelry box where her seed pearl earrings should have been. "Well, then that must not be where you left them. Mom's always saying you need to keep better track of your stuff, and you never listen."

"Well, she's always telling you to be nicer to me, and you never listen to that either."

Bea felt a sudden flash of anger. "Well, maybe if you weren't so annoying I'd be nicer to you!" she yelled.

"Well, maybe if you were nicer, you wouldn't be so annoyed!" Charlie yelled back.

Their dad appeared in the hallway. "Hey, what's going on here?"

"Bea's being mean," Charlie said.

"Charlie's being annoying," Bea said.

Dad smiled and shook his head. "So basically, nothing that hasn't been going on between siblings since the dawn of time. Chill out, you two. I've got to say, I miss the days when you two were best buddies."

⎯⊰○α⊱⎯

As she lay in bed, cuddled up with Devo, Bea couldn't help feeling a little sad about what Dad had said. She did remember a time—not really that long ago—when she and Charlie had been inseparable and hardly squabbled. *Best buddies.* She knew Charlie hadn't changed that much, but she had. Four years ago, even two years ago, she hadn't been annoyed by Charlie, hadn't been embarrassed by her parents, hadn't been so worried about other people's opinions of her. It had been simpler when she was a little girl. But that wasn't the girl she was anymore, and there was no way to go back.

⎯⊰○α⊱⎯

Bea's legs trembled as she stood in the gym in front of a panel made up of the dance team coach, one of the PE teachers, and the beautiful blonde girl she'd seen in the hallway the other day. Bea hadn't danced a single step yet, but she could already feel them judging her.

"So you just moved here?" the dance team coach asked. Lean and elegant, she looked like a grown-up version of one of the current dance team girls.

"That's right," Bea said, wishing the nervous fluttering in her stomach would stop.

"Could you tell me a little bit about your dance experience?" the coach asked.

"I've had seven years of ballet, jazz, and tap," Bea said. "I love to dance." She was afraid this last part sounded stupid, but it was true.

The coach smiled. "All right, let's see what you've got."

It felt like the music was never going to play. Could there be some kind of technical problem? All Bea could hear was the pounding of her heart. But as soon as the music started, Bea's nervousness evaporated. She let the music flow through her and moved where it took her. She felt free. Joyful. When the number ended, she had a smile on her face and saw that the members of the panel were smiling, too. She didn't need anyone to tell her she was in.

As she stepped out of the school building, Bea suddenly felt a sense of hope. She was dancing again. She was on the team. Maybe she had found her place at her new school.

"Hey," a voice behind her said.

She turned around to see the blonde girl who had just been on the panel. She was smiling a dazzling Hollywood smile.

"Welcome to the team," she said. "I'm Olivia."

"Bea." Out of nervousness, Bea held out her hand. Olivia shook it, but then they both laughed because shaking hands was so ridiculous, like they were adults in suits sealing a business deal.

"Hey," Olivia said, "I'm going to meet some of the other girls from the team at the Mighty Bean for coffee. We do our homework there most afternoons. Want to come with?"

Bea had a big smile on her face, even though she hated coffee. "Sure."

The Mighty Bean was dimly lit with exposed brick walls. The aroma of coffee filled the room. Bea thought the place felt very sophisticated.

"Okay, let's introduce you to the posse," Olivia said. "Kayla," she said, nodding toward the girl with black braids, "and Maeve," she said, nodding toward the girl with the chestnut hair, "this is Bea. She's joining the dance team."

"My condolences," Kayla said. "It's exhausting."

"*So* exhausting," Maeve said.

Both girls were drinking big iced coffee drinks, maybe because they were so tired.

At the counter, Bea didn't know what to order, so she asked for the first thing she saw on the menu under the label "non-coffee drinks," something called a Pink Unicorn. When the drink arrived, it was the color of a medicine Bea's mom gave her when her stomach was upset, and topped with whipped cream and rainbow sprinkles.

When she brought her drink to the table, the other girls laughed.

"What did you *order?*" Olivia said. "Pureed princess?"

Bea laughed along. "I don't know what it is, really. Something called a Pink Unicorn."

"Is unicorn, like, an actual ingredient?" Kayla said.

Bea took a sip. It was very sweet, but not bad. Like a milkshake. "It tastes like strawberries."

"So unicorn tastes like strawberries," Maeve said. "Who knew?"

Bea was so happy to be sitting at a table in a café with this glamorous, witty group of girls. Yesterday she had felt lost. Today she felt lucky.

"So for tomorrow we're supposed to read chapters one through three of that novel and answer the questions, right?" Kayla asked.

Olivia rolled her eyes. "You would be the one to bring things around to homework first, wouldn't you?" She opened her laptop. "Hello, Internet!" She typed and stared at the screen for a few moments, then clicked a few times. "Here we go! This site has a detailed summary of each chapter."

It took Bea a couple of minutes to process what was going on. She liked reading, and it had never occurred to her not to read something a teacher assigned. "So are you reading the summaries to help you understand the chapters better?" she asked.

Olivia laughed. "We're reading the summaries *instead* of the chapters, sweetie," she said, like she was explaining something to a much younger child. "When you've been on dance team awhile, you'll understand. Between practice and team meetings and class, there's just some stuff you won't have time for."

Bea had written down answers to the English questions along with the other dance team girls, but now, alone in her room, she decided she would go ahead and read the chapters for real. That way, she would really be prepared for class. And besides, the book, *The Turn of the Screw*, sounded interesting. It was supposed to be a ghost story.

But when she went to get the book, it wasn't where she had left it. She knew she had set the book on her desk with her other homework stuff when she had come home from school. How could it be gone?

This was not good. The English teacher had passed out copies of the book to the class but made a big deal about how they were loaner copies. She had told everybody to take good care of them and return them as soon as the unit on the book was done.

Bea dug through her backpack just in case she had only imagined leaving the book on her desk. It wasn't there. She looked under her bed, on her nightstand and in its drawers, on the dresser and in her drawers. She knew she was looking places it couldn't really be, but she knew it had been in her room. It had to be *somewhere*.

She slid open her closet door and knelt on the floor in front of where her shoes were lined up.

Something caught her eye.

In the back left corner of the closet was a shoebox that didn't belong to her. She pulled it out. It was not new. The cardboard had softened with age, and the box was printed with the words *Jellies, size 6.5.*

She lifted the lid from the box and looked inside. A rush of cold air hit her, and she shivered. She looked down into the box. There was the missing book, along with a dozen of Charlie's trading cards. How had they gotten in here? She took out the book and the cards, and there, at the bottom of the box, were her missing seed pearl earrings.

CHAPTER 4

Bea knew Charlie wasn't awake yet. He could never wake up until after Mom had nagged him for at least thirty minutes, and even then, he still would practically sleepwalk through getting ready for school.

Barefoot, Bea tiptoed into Charlie's room and set the trading cards she'd found the night before on his dresser. Part of her wanted to tell him about the shoebox full of the items that had gone missing, but a bigger part of her thought it would be more fun to have her own secret . . . and to let her brother think he was hallucinating.

It took Bea a long time to decide what to wear for school. Now that she was part of the dance team, she had to make an impression. She finally settled on a pink top and white skinny jeans and the newly found seed pearl earrings. She decided to wear her hair loose around her shoulders because that was the way Olivia wore hers. She wished she had real quality makeup to wear instead of the cheap drugstore kind she could afford. Maybe she could sneak into her mom's bathroom and borrow just a teensy bit of her good mascara.

"Charlie! You need to get up!" she heard her mom call from downstairs. If her mom was downstairs and her dad was out for his morning run, that meant the coast was clear. She tiptoed into her parents' bedroom, then into their bathroom. She opened the black patent leather case where her mom kept her makeup and grabbed a tube of mascara. She tried to brush some onto her lashes quickly, then blinked and ended up with what looked like a black eye. She washed her face and tried again, this time doing better. It definitely went on smoother than the kind she was usually stuck using, and it made her lashes look both darker and longer. The stuff ought to be good. Her mom paid forty dollars a tube for it.

Bea tiptoed out of her parents' room, feeling pretty sure her crime had gone undetected.

"Hey, Bea," Charlie called when she walked past his room. "Wanna hear something weird?"

"If it's coming from you, it's got to be weird," Bea said, though she knew exactly what he was about to say.

"Remember my missing trading cards? When I got up this morning, they were on my dresser!"

"Well, that must have been where you left them," Bea said.

"But it wasn't! They weren't there when I went to bed last night."

Bea shook her head. It was definitely the right decision not to tell him about finding the box. This was much more fun. "Maybe the stress of the move has been too much for you."

Charlie rolled his eyes.

Bea's mom served whole-grain gingerbread pancakes for breakfast. When she sat down at the table across from Bea, she said, "Beatrice, are you wearing my mascara? Your lashes look bolder than usual."

Mom only called her Beatrice when she had done something wrong.

"A little, yes. You're supposed to wear makeup when you're on dance team." Bea tried to look busy pouring agave nectar on her pancake.

"You're supposed to wear makeup when you perform, yes," her mom said, cradling her cup of coffee in two hands. "Are you performing today?"

"No, just practicing."

"I see," Mom said. "And did you get the mascara from my bathroom?"

"I didn't take it. I borrowed it," Bea said, still not looking up.

"Hmm. Generally, when people borrow things, don't they ask first?" Mom sipped her coffee.

"Yes," Bea said. "But I was afraid you'd say no."

"I might've," Mom said. "But now that you're wearing it, I think it looks nice. I think you should keep it as long as you don't act all sneaky and weird about it."

Bea let out a grateful sigh. "Okay. Thanks, Mom."

Mom smiled. "I like the mascara. It makes your eyes pop."

"That sounds gross," Charlie said. "Like she looks like a Chihuahua. They have pop eyes."

Mom laughed. "I don't mean your sister looks like a Chihuahua. Though Chihuahuas are cute, too. Just in a different way."

Bea's family had the strangest conversations. But she was getting to wear better mascara, and at least that was something.

⊰○⊱

"Those white jeans you have on today are super cute," Olivia said. Bea was sitting with her and Kayla and

Maeve in the cafeteria. The dance team girls, Bea noticed, grazed from the cafeteria's salad bar for lunch. She had brought a packed lunch from home—today it was an almond-butter-and-honey sandwich and carrots and hummus. She needed to ask her parents if she could start bringing lunch money instead so she could eat with the rest of the team. The salad bar would be a hard sell, though, since she was pretty sure the vegetables weren't organic.

"Thanks," Bea said. "Hopefully I won't spill anything on them. That's always the danger of wearing white."

"I like that mascara, too," Kayla said. "It looks nice. We'll have to work with you on how to do your makeup for performances. We paint it on pretty thick."

"Yeah," Maeve said, "and we use glitter hairspray, too. It's a pain to wash out, but it looks great in the lights."

"Hi." Bea looked up to see a girl standing by their table. Her hair was dyed fuchsia, and she was wearing a sack-like black dress with black-and-white-striped tights. "I'm guessing I didn't make the dance team," she said.

"You're guessing right," Olivia said with a smile on her face as if she were giving good news instead of bad.

"Okay, whatever," the girl said. "But I still feel

like I could bring something new to your routines."

"If by *new* you mean *weird*, then sure," Olivia said.

Kayla and Maeve laughed.

"Well, provincial people make provincial choices," the girl said. "But I'm still going to try out again next year. Better luck next time, right?"

"You'll definitely need it," Olivia said. "Why are you even talking to us? Shouldn't you be hanging out with your spooky friends who look like they're in a cult?"

"You guys are the cult," the girl said, and walked away.

"A cult you're not cool enough to join!" Olivia said to the girl's back.

Maeve and Kayla laughed even harder. Bea wondered if she should laugh, too.

After the girl was gone, Bea asked, "Who's she?"

"That's Sophie," Olivia said. "This is her second year going out for dance team and getting turned down. She ought to get a clue."

"She does *modern* dance," Kayla said. "Weird stuff where you stomp around barefoot."

"Plus," Maeve said, "she wears those baggy dresses because she's fat. She's never going to be dance team material."

Bea felt a little prickle of anxiety in her stomach.

Sophie didn't look fat to her, and so what if she was? Her parents had always told her that different people looked different ways, and it didn't matter. Also, what was so bad about modern dance? Bea had taken a modern dance class the year before, and she had liked it. It felt so much freer than ballet, and it was fun to dance barefoot.

But she had just gotten her non-bare foot in the door with the dance team, so she wasn't going to argue with them. She wanted Olivia and Kayla and Maeve to like her, and besides, maybe there was more to the story with Sophie than she knew. Maybe Sophie had done something to Olivia or one of the girls, something bad enough to deserve their mean treatment. But even as Bea thought this, there was still a nagging voice in the back of her mind asking, *Does anybody deserve to be talked to that way?*

⬩∘○∘⬩

Bea lay in bed, but she was having trouble sleeping. There was something about the new house that didn't feel restful to her. Maybe it was that her room was always too cold or that the weird grape bubble-gum smell had never quite gone away. Or maybe it was just that she hadn't gotten to the point of thinking of this house as home yet. If she woke up in the middle of the night, she was always disoriented about where she was, and she still had to think to find her way to the bathroom.

You're home, you're safe. You're home, you're safe, Bea told herself over and over in her head. *You're home, you're safe, you're . . .* until finally the comforting message and the repetition soothed her to sleep.

She was awoken by a crash.

She sat up. The sound had come from the direction of her dresser. Her jewelry box had fallen to the floor.

Next to the box, a girl crawled on her hands and knees, scrambling to pick up the scattered jewelry.

Bea rubbed her eyes, then looked again to make sure she was really seeing what she thought she was seeing.

The girl was still there.

"Um . . . excuse me?" Bea said. It was a stupid thing to say. This girl was an intruder in Bea's room; she should be demanding to know who this girl was. Was she a robber, and if so, wasn't it strange for her to be around Bea's own age?

The girl started and looked up. "I'm sorry!" she said, sounding strangely bubbly given the situation. "I didn't mean to wake you up. I accidentally knocked over your jewelry box. I am such a klutz!"

The girl stood up. Her long brown hair was curly, overly styled, and topped with a big pink bow. She was wearing a puffy white sweater decorated with huge pink polka dots and a matching short pink skirt. Her pink shoes, worn with white ankle socks, seemed to be made of shiny plastic.

"Who are you?" Bea asked, finally finding the right words. "And what are you doing in my room?"

The girl smiled. Her lips were gooey with pink lip gloss the same shade as her pink earrings. If she was a robber, she was an exceptionally color-coordinated one. "I'm Kimberly," she said. "My friends call me Kimmie. And this was my room way before it was yours."

"What? I don't understand. Am I dreaming?"

"If you really want to find out, I'll be happy to pinch you. But I've got to warn you—I pinch *hard!*" Kimmie made a crablike pinching motion with both hands and giggled.

"What do you mean that this was your room before it was mine?" Bea said, struggling to find the right questions to ask to make sense of this bizarre situation.

Kimmie sat down on the foot of Bea's bed, though the mattress didn't squeak or give. It was as though no weight had been placed on it at all. The smell of grape bubble gum grew stronger, and Bea noticed the steady chewing motion of Kimmie's jaw.

"This is my house and my room," Kimmie said. "I grew up here. I'm still here and will always be as long as there's a me." She giggled again. "I rhymed! I'm always here, Bea. I just don't always let you see me. I rhymed again!"

Bea's confusion was replaced by fear. "Do you mean that you hide?"

"I guess you could call it that. I'm a very good hider. Watch."

Kimmie closed her eyes and was gone. In astonishment, Bea looked around at the now-empty room—or was it?

"Over here!" Kimmie's voice called. She reappeared sitting crisscross applesauce on top of Bea's dresser.

Bea's mouth was hanging open. It took a few seconds for her to gather her thoughts enough to speak. "But you were here, then you were gone. And now you're there!"

"Awesome job keeping up. You're a smart girl, huh?"

"I—I guess," Bea said, still unable to believe she was having this conversation. "So, Kimmie, are you . . . a ghost?"

Kimmie crinkled her nose. "I don't totally love the g-word. But I do love that you called me Kimmie, because that's what my friends call me! We're going to be friends, okay?"

"Okay," Bea said, but the word sounded as unsure as she felt. Was she agreeing to be friends with a dead person? Because if Kimmie was a ghost, that meant she was dead, didn't it? Asking her if she was dead seemed rude somehow. "But here's the thing. I think that maybe you took some stuff from me and hid it away in the closet. Friends don't take stuff from each other without asking."

Bea realized she was echoing her mom's words from this morning. But the mascara wasn't like the earrings, was it?

Kimmie looked thoughtful. "The closet's where I always kept my secrets. Sometimes friends borrow things from each other, right?"

"Yes, but they ask first."

"Ask first," Kimmie said. "Okay, I got it." She slid down from the dresser and returned to the foot of the bed. "I'm not really a thief," she said, dangling her legs over the edge of the bed. "It's just that being here like this, I'm so alone. Sometimes if I have something real to look at or to touch—it just makes me feel less discon-nected, you know?"

Bea nodded. She knew a little about feeling alone and disconnected from having to move, but the kind of disconnection Kimmie was talking about was something else altogether. "Do you have a family?" Bea asked.

"I did. When I was really *living* here. That was back in the '80s, a long time before you were born."

"Wow," Bea said. "I mean . . . I don't know what to say, you know?"

"Yeah, I know it's weird. I guess if I'd lived, I'd be around your mom's age by now. But I didn't, so I'm around your age instead. That means we can be friends, right?" Kimmie cocked her head and smiled like a kid in a TV show trying to look adorable.

"Yeah, sure. I mean you're a good g—" She almost said *ghost* but then remembered that Kimmie had said she didn't like to use that word. "What I mean is, I can trust you, can't I?"

Kimmie picked up one of Bea's pillows and hugged it to her chest. "Absolutely! You can totally trust me."

"Okay, good." Bea looked over at her alarm clock. Three a.m.! "Kimmie, it was great talking to you, but I'm going to have to get some sleep if I'm going to go to school in the morning."

Kimmie made a *yuck* face. "One of the only good things about being in the state I'm in is that I don't have to go to school."

"I still have to."

"Yeah, I get it. I guess I'll disappear for now."

"Where will you go?" Bea asked. She wondered if there was some kind of gathering place for ghosts to hang out.

"Oh, I won't go anywhere. You just won't be able to see me. I can't leave this house."

"You mean you've been in this house since the 1980s?"

Kimmie nodded. "It's so lonely and dull. You can see how I got in the habit of taking things."

"I can," Bea said. She got an idea then and pushed back her blanket. "Hang on for a second. Don't disappear yet." Bea got out of bed, went to her jewelry box, and took out the seed pearl earrings. "Here," she said, "you can borrow these. Because we're friends."

Kimmie took them and smiled.

CHAPTER 5

The music was flowing through her. Bea, Olivia, Kayla, and Maeve were in the front row while the other members of the team danced behind them. It felt amazing to dance with other people, to have her body moving in sync not just with the music, but with all the other girls. As always, when Bea danced, she felt like she wasn't even thinking, that her body just automatically knew how to move. Her heart beat in time with the music's thumping bass. She was happy.

Coach Braden applauded when the music ended. "Great job today, ladies! We're going to tear it up at regionals this year!"

The girls headed for the water fountain. Bea noticed

that the other girls hung back so that Olivia, Kayla, and Maeve could drink first.

"Everybody up for the Mighty Bean?" Olivia asked as they were changing in the locker room.

"Sure," Maeve said. "Coach Braden never gives compliments like that. I feel like we should celebrate."

"It's because of Bea," Olivia said. "We were good last year, but she's given us that little something extra. She's our secret ingredient!"

"Our special sauce," Kayla said.

Bea felt her face warming up from embarrassment, but she couldn't help smiling.

At the Mighty Bean, Bea ordered a coffee drink with chocolate and marshmallow fluff that was supposed to taste like s'mores. No more pink drinks for her. It was pretty good—the chocolate and marshmallow went a long way to disguising the bitterness of the coffee, and pretty soon she started to feel hyper and happy from the jolt of caffeine.

"Ready for me to look up some more chapter summaries?" Maeve asked.

Bea didn't need the chapter summaries because she was reading the book on her own at home. She was enjoying it, actually. But there was no way she was going to admit either of these things to her friends.

"Oh, look who just slunk in," Olivia said under her breath. "The funeral party."

Bea looked toward the door. There was Sophie, wearing a floor-length, high-collared black dress, and a girl with spiky blue hair and ripped black jeans. A pale, skinny, black-clad guy was with them, too, his hair hanging in his face so it was hard to see what he looked like.

"Hey, it's Morticia Addams!" Olivia called at them. "Are those your children, Wednesday and Pugsley?"

"Hey, Barbies," Sophie said.

"We're not Barbies. We just don't turn every day into Halloween," Olivia said.

"Yeah, we'd rather look like somebody's dream, not somebody's nightmare," Maeve said.

"Well, nightmares are in the eye of the beholder," Sophie's guy friend said, and the three of them turned their attention to ordering coffee.

Bea didn't understand why her friends felt the need to pick on Sophie and the other Goth kids. But it wasn't her place to say anything. She loved being part of such a glamorous group, and since she was the group's newest member, she didn't feel like her status was very stable yet.

Bea was stretched out on the couch watching videos on her laptop when her mom came in, looking a little agitated. "Bea, you didn't happen to borrow my silver teardrop-shaped earrings today, did you?" she asked.

"Just because I used your mascara doesn't mean I'm going to start stealing your jewelry," Bea said. "I'd never take something valuable like that without asking."

"I know you wouldn't. It's just so confusing. I know they were in my jewelry drawer."

"You didn't take them off and put them in your bag when you went to the gym, did you?" Bea asked.

"I don't think so, but I'll check my gym bag just to be safe," Mom said.

Bea was pretty sure she knew her mom's earrings weren't in her gym bag. Bea didn't have them, but she had a good idea of who did.

-9OO8-

Kimmie was in the habit of coming to visit after Bea was in bed. Tonight, when she showed up, she was wearing Bea's mom's earrings with her usual pink-and-white outfit.

"My mom was looking for those earrings," Bea said.

Kimmie slipped them off and held them out to her. "You can give them back to her. They're so pretty; I just wanted to wear them for a while."

"How did you get ahold of them when you can't leave this room?" Bea asked, setting the earrings on her nightstand.

Kimmie smiled. "She came in here to put some laundry away. I came up behind her and slipped them right out of her earlobes. She didn't even notice. She just shivered and mumbled that she didn't know why it was always so chilly in here."

Bea shook her head. "Kimmie! You said you weren't going to take anything else without permission."

Kimmie grinned adorably and shrugged. "I know. It's just so boring here. Sometimes I can't resist something new. Or something shiny. Hey, can I put my head on your shoulder?"

"Sure." Bea thought it was kind of weird that Kimmie liked to lie with her head on Bea's shoulder, but she didn't mind it really, and it seemed to make Kimmie happy. She said it made her feel like they were sisters.

For Bea, it felt strange. She could feel Kimmie lying on her, but she didn't have the weight of a living human. She was like a hollow doll.

"So what did you do today?" Kimmie asked. She

always seemed eager to know what was going on beyond the house in which she was trapped.

"Not much," Bea said. "School. Dance team practice. Went out for coffee with my friends."

"We didn't go out for coffee when I was in school," Kimmie said. She was lying on her side next to Bea, curled up in a little ball. "Ice cream or frozen yogurt but never coffee."

"To tell the truth, I like ice cream and frozen yogurt way better than coffee," Bea said. "But Olivia, Kayla, and Maeve drink coffee, so I drink coffee, too." It was funny. In a lot of ways, Bea was more open and honest with Kimmie than she was with her new friends. At school she was always overthinking everything she said or did to try to make a good impression. With Kimmie, she was more her natural self.

"I would never make you drink coffee if you didn't want to," Kimmie said.

Bea laughed. "Thank you. But they don't make me drink it. I'm sure it would be fine if I ordered something else." Although they had made fun of her that first day at the Mighty Bean when she ordered the Pink Unicorn.

"Your new friends at school, are they nice like I am?" Kimmie asked.

Bea thought of Olivia and the others teasing Sophie. "They're nice but in a different way than you are."

Kimmie rolled onto her back and smiled up at Bea. "Different is good. I want to be special. I want to be your best friend, Bea."

Bea made a noncommittal *mmm* sound instead of saying yes or no. Some days she wondered if these long conversations with Kimmie were real or just figments of her imagination. But even if Kimmie were real, could you have a dead person as a best friend?

"So, Kimmie," Bea said, trying to change the subject, "what kinds of things did you like to do when you, you know, lived here?" She tried to phrase things so she didn't say *when you were alive.*

"Just usual stuff. I liked to watch music videos. Hang out at the mall, go to the arcade, that kind of thing. *Ms. Pac-Man* was my favorite game. I was totally awesome at it."

"I've played that game before," Bea said. "Once when we were on vacation we went to a retro arcade."

"You know what I wish?" Kimmie said. "I wish I could go to the mall with you. We could shop for clothes and get ice cream and go to the arcade and play all the games. I might even let you win at *Ms. Pac-Man,* but probably not."

"There's not an arcade at the mall anymore," Bea said.

"Oh." Kimmie sounded disappointed.

"So when you were alive, did you go to the mall with your friends?" Bea hoped she could cheer Kimmie up by making her remember some fun times.

Kimmie's face clouded over, and her eyes darkened. "Not much. I didn't have a nice friend like you back then, Bea. Some girls . . . weren't nice to me. I didn't like that. I didn't like that at all."

CHAPTER 6

Bea knew she wasn't sleeping enough. During the day her brain felt fuzzy around the edges, and she had to work hard not to doze off during her more boring classes. Dance team practice exhausted her, and afterward, she found that she really *needed* the big coffee she ordered at the Mighty Bean, even if all the chocolate and caramel and whipped cream still didn't quite hide the bitter taste, because she knew when she got home there would still be homework and chores and taking a shower and laying out her clothes for the next exhausting day.

Bea also knew the reason she wasn't sleeping enough. Every night, within five minutes of when she turned out the light, Kimmie appeared. They always talked for at least two hours, and when Bea started yawning and saying she needed to get some rest for school, Kimmie would get all upset and say that talking to Bea was the only thing she had to look forward to.

Last night when Bea had said she needed to go to bed, Kimmie had said, "I'm so sad I could cry, but I can't make tears." Bea loved the time she spent with Kimmie—how many people had the opportunity to be friends with a ghost?—but she wished Kimmie could be around during hours she was actually supposed to be awake.

And Kimmie could be kind of needy and demanding, but how could you blame her? She was trapped inside a house, seemingly for all time to come, and Bea was all she had.

Tonight, though, Bea knew she would probably get no sleep at all. At least it would be for a fun reason—she had invited Olivia over tonight for a sleepover. Both Kayla and Maeve were busy with family stuff, and so when Bea had asked Olivia over on impulse, Bea was shocked when she said yes.

And if there was one thing that was true about sleepovers, it was that nobody ever got any sleep.

Bea found her mom in the kitchen chopping vegetables. "Hey, I found these," Bea said, setting the silver teardrop earrings on the kitchen counter.

"Where in the world were they?" her mom asked.

"In my room under the dresser," Bea said. "They must've fallen out when you were putting laundry away or something."

"Both of them? At the same time?" Mom said, looking up from the mushrooms she was slicing. "It would be weird for that to happen without my noticing."

"Well, that's where I found them," Bea said.

"Huh." Her mom went back to slicing. "Maybe I took them off for some reason and forgot about them. I swear, ever since this move, I feel like I've gotten so absent-minded. I don't feel like I can keep up with anything."

Bea decided to let this go without comment and change the subject. "Olivia will be here at six."

"So you keep telling me," her mom said. "We're doing a pizza bar. Everybody gets their own individual-sized pizza and can pick out the toppings they want, and then I'll bake them."

"You got pepperoni, right? Because that's Olivia's favorite." As the time drew closer to Olivia's visit, Bea was getting more and more nervous. She had to get this right.

"Yes, I got pepperoni, even though it's highly processed and gross."

"Thanks, Mom. Do you want me to sweep in the living room?"

Her mom shrugged. "If you think it needs it."

Bea's parents were casual about housework, which was usually fine with Bea, but right now, she was looking at the house through Olivia's eyes and saw that things weren't as neat and clean as they could be. Looking at Mom through Olivia's eyes left some room for improvement, too. Her mom was wearing ratty old jeans and a black T-shirt with a skull on it that was the mascot of some old band she liked. Her feet were bare, and her toenails were painted blue.

"Is that what you're planning on wearing?" Bea asked.

"What, you want me to dress for dinner?" her mom said. "This is my own house, Bea. I'm not going to put on a ball gown just because your fancy friend is coming over."

Bea decided to pick her battles. She went to get the broom.

───◦◦◦───

"This house is wild. I love it," Olivia said as she sat at the dinner table with Bea and her family. "This pizza's really good, too. My mom's on a diet right now, so every night all we have is grilled chicken and steamed vegetables. It's getting super boring, but when Mom goes on a diet, we all go on a diet."

"Makes sense," Bea's mom said, lifting a slice of pizza to her mouth. "Why suffer alone?"

Bea had to admit that her parents were on their best behavior. They didn't bring out Bea's baby pictures or tell any embarrassing stories about when she was little. And luckily, Charlie was over at a friend's house, so she didn't have to worry about any little brother weirdness.

After dinner was over, once Bea and Olivia were alone in Bea's room, Olivia said, "Your parents are cool."

"Thanks," Bea said. She was surprised because she usually thought of them as odd and embarrassing.

"They're much more relaxed than my parents. Everything with them has to be just so. Perfect house, perfect yard, perfect kid. That would be me, by the way. No pressure there, right?" Olivia stretched out on Bea's bed. She was even wearing perfectly matched pajamas, in contrast to Bea's T-shirt and sweatpants. "I like your cat, too. I can't have a pet because Mom says they're messy."

"Well, she's not wrong. Devo is pretty messy," Bea

said. "I wish he'd come in here and hang out so you can pet him."

Back at the old house, Devo had slept with Bea every night. But since they had moved, he didn't want to come into her room, and slept with her parents instead. It kind of hurt Bea's feelings not to have his warm furriness to snuggle with at night.

"Me too," Olivia said. "Dad won't let me have a pet because he worries that it would aggravate my asthma, but I think he's just being overprotective. Sometimes parents need to just back off, you know?"

"Yeah," Bea said. Though when she thought about it, her parents probably let her get away with more than a lot of kids' parents.

"I'm so glad you moved here," Olivia said. "I mean, I love Kayla and Maeve, but I've known them literally since kindergarten. We can finish each other's sentences, and nothing either of them ever did could surprise me. But you . . . you're full of surprises. It's fun having a new friend."

Bea felt herself blushing. Why was that always her reaction to compliments? It was like she got embarrassed at the compliment and then got embarrassed again because she was blushing. "Thanks. I like having you as a new friend, too. And Kayla and Maeve are great."

"Yeah," Olivia said. "We cool girls have got to stick together. You've been here long enough to notice some of the losers that go to our school. No fashion sense, no social skills, no nothing. Like that nerd in math class who wears those ugly vests, or that freak who keeps trying out for dance team."

"Sophie?" Bea asked. She didn't really want to talk about Sophie.

"Yeah. Oh, the other day I called her *Sofa* because she's as wide as a sofa. The whole class loved it—isn't that hilarious?"

"Sure," Bea said, though there was no way that Sophie was comparable in size to any piece of furniture. "I guess I don't understand why you guys tease her so much, though." She was nervous as soon as she said it that she would make Olivia mad.

But Olivia smiled. "It's not really teasing. It's for her own good. Somebody's got to tell her the truth about herself, or how will she ever improve? Between you and me, though, I'm afraid she's a lost cause, doomed to go through life in those baggy black dresses looking like a big, fat spider." Olivia's cell phone pinged, and her eyes brightened as she looked at the notification. "Hey, they just put up the new season of *The Rumor Mill*. You want to binge it?"

"Sure," Bea said, grateful that the conversation had steered away from Sophie. She had never watched the show, but it was popular at school—Olivia and Kayla and Maeve talked about it all the time.

They sprawled on Bea's bed and watched three episodes on Bea's laptop. It was pretty entertaining, Bea thought, but she never understood why high school students on TV shows were always played by good-looking thirty-year-olds. No one really looked like that. After the first three episodes, the girls went down to the kitchen for some of the oatmeal peanut butter cookies Bea's mom had made. They went back to Bea's room and watched another episode, but started yawning soon after.

By the time Bea unrolled an old futon cushion and outfitted it with a pillow and a blanket, Olivia was already under the covers in Bea's bed. "I guess I'll take the floor," Bea said. Olivia didn't argue, but Bea guessed it made sense. Olivia was used to having nice things. Sleeping on the floor would definitely be something she'd look down on.

"Is there any way I could get an extra blanket?" Olivia asked. "It's freezing in here."

"Sure," Bea said, going to her closet to get a blanket off the shelf. "This is the coldest room in the house."

"It is. And it smells like grape air freshener."

Bea decided to let that one go. What was she supposed to say? *Actually, you're smelling a ghost's bubble gum?*

It took Bea a while to relax, but in no time, she heard Olivia's slow, even breathing. She sat up to catch a glimpse of her friend sleeping. Olivia's golden hair was spread out across the pillow. Her long eyelashes were fanned out, and her full pink lips were slightly parted. She looked like a princess in a fairy tale. Like Sleeping Beauty. Bea wondered what it would be like to be that pretty.

She decided she was lucky enough just to have someone that pretty who was willing to be friends with her. Smiling a little, she closed her eyes and went to sleep.

Bea was awakened by the sound of choking and gasping coming from her bed. She threw off the covers and sprang to her feet. Kimmie was straddling Olivia's sleeping body. One of her hands was over Olivia's mouth and was pinching her nostrils shut. The other hand was tight around Olivia's throat.

Olivia's eyes were closed, and strange gags and gurgles emitted from her throat.

"Kimmie, stop that!" Bea cried.

Kimmie kept her hands where they were, but turned to look at Bea, her face a mask of fury. "How could you bring her here? You're *my* friend, and this is *my* room!"

"Olivia's my friend, too! Let go of her!"

"She's too mean to be a good friend. I won't let her go until you promise you won't let her stay here again."

How long did it take for a person to choke to death? "Yes, I promise, I promise!" Bea said frantically.

"And you have to say I'm your best friend, not her," Kimmie said. Her fingers were no longer holding Olivia's nose shut, but she hadn't relinquished her grip on her throat.

"Okay, you're my best friend!" Bea said, sobbing in fear.

"That's much better," Kimmie said. "Get rid of her." She took both her hands off Olivia and disappeared.

Olivia coughed and sputtered, and Bea ran to her side. "Are you okay?" she asked.

Olivia reached up and touched her throat. "I must have had an asthma attack in my sleep." She took a deep, rattling breath. "That's weird. I haven't had one in ages. Maybe my dad is right. Maybe cat fur does aggravate it."

"Maybe so," Bea said. She couldn't shake the image of Kimmie strangling Olivia, of the look of rage on her face. "We should probably call your parents to pick you up. It's not safe for you to be here."

CHAPTER 7

Now Bea truly was exhausted. Olivia had said she wanted to stay the night despite Bea urging her to go. Bea had stayed awake for the rest of the night watching over her to make sure Kimmie didn't come back. It was the only way she could think of to keep Olivia safe.

Bea had dragged her way through the next day, and now that it was bedtime again, her body ached for rest. But she couldn't sleep yet. She needed to talk to Kimmie.

As usual, Kimmie appeared on the foot of the bed just a few minutes after Bea turned off the light. "What's buzzin', honey-Bea?" she asked, all smiles.

Bea sat up in bed, furious. Was Kimmie just going

to act like nothing happened? "How can you be all friendly and casual when you tried to kill my friend?"

Kimmie rolled her eyes as if Bea were being ridiculous. "She didn't belong here. This room is yours and mine. She was an intruder."

"She was not an intruder! I invited her."

"Well, *I* didn't. And you didn't ask me if you could invite her."

"I have to ask your permission to ask a friend over?"

"I don't think that's unreasonable," Kimmie said. "It's my room and my house, too, you know."

Bea couldn't get the image out of her head of Kimmie straddling Olivia's sleeping body, choking the life out of her. "Kimmie, you almost killed her."

Kimmie shrugged. "But I didn't."

"That was only because I stopped you."

Kimmie studied her pink-polished fingernails like she was bored. "I could've stopped any time I wanted to. I just wasn't sure I wanted to yet."

Bea felt a chill race down her spine at how cold Kimmie sounded. She realized she was hugging her knees to her chest in an attempt to put some physical distance between her and the ghost girl. "Kimmie, I think I'm afraid of you," she whispered.

All at once, the chill was gone, and Kimmie giggled. "But, Bea, that's so silly! How could you possibly be scared of somebody who just wants to be your best friend?"

"Well, if she tries to murder my other friends—"

"Okay," Kimmie said, her voice pleading. "I admit it. I got jealous. I know you have other friends when you go to school or other places out in the world. But I *can't* go out in the world. I just have you. Just you and our room. And I don't think it's unfair to ask that when you spend time in your room, you spend it with me. Does that make sense?"

It did, in a way. But in other ways, it made Bea uncomfortable. "I understand what you're saying," Bea said. This was what her dad always said when somebody said something he didn't agree with but he didn't want to get into an argument. "Anyway, Kimmie, I didn't get any sleep last night, so I really should go to bed."

"You living people, always sleeping or eating," Kimmie said. "So high maintenance." She gave Bea a pat on the leg. "Okay, I'll go, but first you have to promise that you're not mad at me."

"I promise that I'm not mad at you," Bea said. Did she mean it? She guessed it was true. She didn't feel that mad at Kimmie. What she did feel was scared of her.

"Okay, I'll let you get some sleep," Kimmie said, and disappeared.

But she still must have been in the room, right? Just because you didn't see Kimmie, it didn't mean that she wasn't there. It was a long time until Bea slept.

The sleep that Bea finally did get was fitful and troubled by disturbing dreams of hands around her throat, of fingers pinching her nostrils closed. She woke up gasping for breath. Outside her window, the sky was the soft gray of early morning. It was Sunday, so she didn't have to be up early, but here she was anyway, her eyes wide open, her stomach knotted in anxiety, her mind filled with thoughts of Kimmie. There would be no more sleeping. She turned on her lamp.

Bea looked around her room. But was it her room or Kimmie's? Kimmie certainly seemed to see the room as hers. Kimmie seemed to see Bea as hers, too. Kimmie also seemed all too willing to destroy anyone who might come between her and her "best friend."

It was strange. Bea knew very little of what Kimmie's life had been like back when she was alive. She tossed out little crumbs of information, like what songs or music videos or arcade games she liked, but never anything meaningful or a story about her life. Instead, she liked to hear Bea talk about her life and her days, like she was taking in some of Bea's energy with every story.

A memory came to Bea in a flash. The box of missing things. Kimmie had said something about the closet being where she had always kept her secrets. Bea got out of bed and slid open the closet door.

The old shoebox was there, and Bea peeked inside it. There was a pair of pink socks she had assumed the dryer had eaten and a tortoiseshell hair barrette she hardly ever used. No harm in letting Kimmie keep those things. It wasn't like they were family heirlooms.

But then she saw something in the closet itself. In the back right corner, some of the drywall was missing, and an opening had been covered by a loose board. What was back there? She pulled the board away and reached inside the hole, fearing mice or rats—or worse. But what she found was a book. It was small, with a pink fake leather cover decorated with puffy clouds and rainbows.

When Bea opened it up, the first page was printed with the words *This Diary Belongs To* . . . with blank spaces for the name and the date. In big, loopy handwriting, the blanks were filled with *Kimberly Carr* and *1985*. In various spots on the page in the same handwriting were the warnings *Hands off! For my eyes only* and *If you read this, you'll be sorry!*

Bea shivered. Had the room grown colder? She

hoped these warnings were just intended for family members back when Kimmie was alive. Even so, it didn't feel quite safe to be reading the diary in her room with an invisible Kimmie there watching her. She knew from the quiet of the house that everybody else was still asleep, so she could still have some privacy if she took the diary downstairs.

She sat down on the couch to read. Devo jumped up to get in her lap, but then sniffed the diary, emitted a low growl, and jumped right back down.

"You are the weirdest cat," Bea muttered. She opened up the diary and started to read:

November 12, 1985

Grounded again, this time for sneaking out of the house in the middle of the night. I wasn't doing anything bad. But sometimes I wake up and feel like an animal trapped in a cage and all I can think is get out, get out, get out. So I got out and I got caught and now I'm stuck inside "for my own good." I have the strictest parents in the world. I am not a little kid anymore and I'm tired of being treated like one. The other day Dad called me Pooh Bear in front of some other kids when he came to pick me up from school. I have never been so humiliated.

There were lots of entries like this, Kimmie venting about how mad she was at her parents, at teachers, at other kids. There was one girl in particular whose name came up again and again:

Today Christi Benjamin spilled grape juice all over my new pink-and-white sweater. It was purple grape juice, too, not the white kind. She said it was an accident, but she laughed at me when she did it and so did her mean friends. I've had the sweater soaking for hours, but the stain won't come out. On top of that, at the last school dance, Andrew Sutton asked Christi to dance instead of me. The world would be a better place without Christi Benjamin in it.

But it was the last entry in the diary that chilled Bea and made her understand why Devo had growled at the book:

December 5, 1986

Christi Benjamin is in my chemistry class. Sometimes in chemistry labs accidents happen. Chemical spills. Explosions. When Christi spilled the grape juice, which never came out of my pink-and-white *sweater, she said it was an accident. I'll show her what a real accident looks like. I said the world would be a better place without Christi Benjamin in it. I'm going to make that happen. I'm going to fix things.*

Bea flipped page after page, desperate to find out what had happened, but after that entry, there was nothing but blank pages.

Bea's chest felt tight and her palms were sweaty. Had Kimmie really done something terrible to the girl who picked on her, or was the diary partially fictional, just her way of blowing off steam when somebody made her mad? Somebody making Kimmie mad was something that seemed to happen often.

Bea didn't want to go back to her room, maybe not ever, but she did want to look up Kimmie's name online just to make sure that the threats in the diary were all talk. She went into her mom's office and logged on to the desktop computer that her mom used for her graphic design business. She figured she'd probably have to narrow her search, but for starters, she typed "Kimberly Carr" into a search engine.

There was no need to narrow her search. The first article that came up had the headline "Explosion at Local High School Leaves One Dead, Two Injured."

Another read, "Local Teen Allegedly Kills Parents After Leaving Site of Explosion."

Before Bea could even bring herself to click on an article, she felt her stomach heave, and she threw up violently into the wastebasket.

With a shaking hand, Bea clicked on the first article, which showed two school pictures of smiling, big-haired girls. One was Kimmie, and the other was Christi Benjamin, who had died when a Bunsen burner in the chemistry lab exploded in her face. Was this the "accident" that Kimmie had referred to in her diary? The "accident" Kimmie had planned in the house where Bea was living and where Kimmie, though not exactly living, was still a presence?

Bea tried to read the article, but she was so panicked that the words swam before her eyes. Still, she picked up the gist of what happened. There had been something wrong with the Bunsen burner that Christi and her two lab partners used. The chemistry teacher said that he had checked everything that morning, that the only way the equipment could have malfunctioned was if someone had tampered with it.

Bea was having a hard time processing the words in the article. *"The bodies of Jeremy and Holly Carr, both apparently poisoned, were found at the couple's home on*

1276 Beechwood Drive. A pan of brownies, some of which had been consumed by Mr. and Mrs. Carr, was analyzed and found to contain a high quantity of a commercially available rat poison . . ."

The list of Kimberly Carr–related articles spanned hundreds of pages. Bea clicked on something called "The Serial Bowl: A Blog About My Favorite Serial Killers." The blog's tone was light and gossipy like it was about pop stars instead of murderers and included a list titled:

MY FAVORITE QUOTES FROM KIDDIE KILLER KIMBERLY CARR

"Christi Benjamin? Sure I killed her. She had bullied me mercilessly every day of my life since third grade. And I know I wasn't the only one she picked on. I was doing the world a favor. Now the only place she can bully people is in Hell."

"My parents were cruel, terrible people, and I only killed them because I snapped after years of mistreatment. It was always rules, rules, rules with them, and they would never buy me the things a girl needs. Now that they're gone, I'm hoping I can live with my aunt and uncle, who let me do what I want and have lots of money to buy me things."

There were other quotes, but Bea had seen enough. She clicked on one more newspaper headline from a week after the murders. It read, "Teen Murderer Accidentally Falls to her Death Attempting to Escape Juvenile Detention Center."

It was strange. If Kimmie had died trying to escape the juvenile detention center, then why had her ghost ended up back at her house? Was it a matter of returning to the scene of the crime?

Bea remembered that when her class had studied Greek mythology in fifth grade, they had read about Pandora, who, out of curiosity, opened a forbidden box. When she lifted the lid, all the evil in the world that had been safely trapped flew out to contaminate the earth. Bea was pretty sure that opening Kimmie's diary hadn't been that different from opening Pandora's box.

CHAPTER 8

O n Monday morning, before class started, Bea sat in the school library at one of the computers. There had to be somebody who could help cleanse the house of Kimmie's presence, but what was she supposed to type into the search engine to find such a person? *Ghostbuster?* Ha ha. *Exorcist* didn't seem right; Kimmie was evil, but not a demon. Finally, she settled on *paranormal investigator.*

Of course, even if she could find a reliable paranormal expert, she wasn't sure she'd have enough money to pay such a person. And all the money had to come from her. Her family couldn't know about it. A couple of weeks ago she had tried to talk to her mom about all the items that had disappeared since they had moved. "Mom," she had asked, "do you think something could be *wrong* with the house?" Her mom had looked at her like she wasn't even speaking English. Rational people didn't really believe in ghosts, and there was no way to convince them otherwise.

Bea scrolled for a little, rejecting one business with really high rates, and another that was halfway across the country. Finally, she found a site for a business called Peace Restored Paranormal Investigators. The name definitely described the result Bea wanted. The website showed a picture of a middle-aged woman with blunt cut brown hair and glasses who looked like she could be a therapist or a librarian. She looked trustworthy. Bea saved the number in her phone and went to find a place to make the call.

The second-floor girls' bathroom was empty. Bea locked herself in a stall and dialed the number.

"Hi, this is Amy," a cheerful voice answered.

"Um . . . I was actually calling for Peace Restored Paranormal Investigators?"

"Yes, I am a paranormal investigator." Her voice became much more serious. "Describe your situation, please."

As quickly as Bea could, because the bell for first period would ring soon, she told Amy about the house, about Kimmie, and about what Kimmie was like both in life and in ghost form.

"Fascinating," Amy said. "Well, let me tell you . . . I'm not like those guys who come in with all kinds of fancy equipment and antagonize the ghost. What I do is a house cleansing. I treat the ghost with respect, but I ask it to leave and then make sure it does."

"That sounds perfect," Bea said. "How soon can you do it?"

"Well, let me look at my schedule and see what I can rearrange," Amy said. "Oh, you're in luck. I could fit you in this afternoon."

Bea thought for a minute. How could she do this so her parents and Charlie wouldn't know? Charlie's dorky card playing club met after school this afternoon, and her mom had yoga from four until five. Her dad generally didn't get home until six at the earliest. "Could you do four o'clock? I need you to come when my parents aren't home. They don't believe in this kind of stuff."

"Many people don't, and it is to their detriment," Amy said. "Four o'clock it is."

"Oh, and I guess I should ask how much you charge," Bea said.

"How much are you offering?"

Bea thought about the birthday money she had

been saving, plus the money from last week's allowance. "Fifty dollars?"

"Fifty dollars it is."

⸙

"You seem super distracted today," Olivia told Bea as the girls picked at their salads at lunch.

"I'm sorry," Bea said. "What were you saying?"

"We were saying," Olivia said, spearing a piece of broccoli, "that we're going to Adora at the mall after school today to look at makeup. With our first real performance coming up, we've got to make sure we look fabulous."

"And we promised to help you with stage makeup," Maeve said. "Come on, I know a perfect pencil for those brows."

"I'd love to, but I can't," Bea said, racking her brain for a credible lie. "I've got an appointment this afternoon. A dentist's appointment. A cleaning."

Olivia frowned, and Kayla looked at her with narrowed eyes. "Are you sure you're okay?"

"I'm fine," Bea said. "Going to the dentist just makes me really nervous."

"Well, you could always cancel and let us work on your makeup instead," Olivia said, spearing another piece of broccoli. "You could use it. You're as pale as a ghost."

⚭OO⚭

The doorbell rang at exactly 4 p.m. Bea was downstairs, too nervous even to go up and put her backpack in her room. Devo had been sitting on her lap but ran to hide when she jumped up. Bea opened the door to find Amy looking exactly like her picture on the website except that she was wearing leggings and a fuzzy sweatshirt. Standing beside her was a pale, pimply-faced boy who was wearing a T-shirt for a metal band and didn't look much older than Bea.

"Hello," Amy said. "We're here for the cleansing. I am Amy Moreland, licensed paranormal investigator, and this is my son, Jared, who'll be assisting me."

"'Sup?" said Jared, not even making eye contact with Bea. He didn't appear to be any more excited than any other teenager who had been asked to run some kind of errand with his mom.

"Come in," Bea said.

As soon as they were inside, Amy started looking around and, it seemed, sniffing the air. "So your room is the main center of activity?" she asked.

"Yes," Bea said.

"Take me there."

The three of them headed upstairs and stood in Bea's room. "Definitely a cold spot in here," Amy said.

"Smells like grape bubble gum," Jared muttered.

"It always does," Bea said.

"Spirit, I sense your presence," Amy said, speaking loudly so her voice filled up the room. "I am told your name is Kimberly, is that correct?"

The three of them stood there awkwardly waiting for something to happen. Nothing did.

"Kimberly," Amy continued finally, "I am going to ask you to leave. Will you go peacefully?"

As if someone had swatted it, the jewelry box on Bea's dresser fell to the floor with a crash.

"Whoa," Jared said.

"Well," Amy said, "I think you've just given us an answer." She looked at Bea and Jared. "Let's go back downstairs."

Once they were in the living room, Amy unpacked her tote bag and showed Bea the contents. "White sage, sea salt, and a bell."

"Oh-kay," Bea said, trying to sound like these three objects made some kind of sense to her.

"The sage and sea salt will cleanse the house of negative energy. Jared will be my bell ringer," Amy said. "The vibrations attract the spirit and persuade it to exit the home."

Bea nodded. All of this seemed like a lot of hocus-pocus, but a month ago she hadn't believed in ghosts either. Clearly there were lots of things that were possible that she had never considered before.

Amy wandered from room to room in the house, scattering sea salt in the doorways and on the windowsills. She left the front door and the back door wide open, and Bea put Devo in his cat carrier so he wouldn't dart out, which made him furious. She tossed a few cat treats in to mollify him.

Then things got weird. Well, weirder. Amy lit the bundle of white sage on fire and started waving it in the air, and Jared followed her, ringing the bell, which had a surprisingly low, deep tone. Amy was singing or chanting softly, too, but the words were not in English. Bea sat on the couch nervously as Amy roamed through every room in the house, waving the sage and chanting, with Jared ringing the bell behind her.

Bea was getting a little anxious about the time. Her mom would be home from yoga in half an hour. How could Bea possibly explain things if Amy and Jared were still here?

After a few minutes, though, Amy came to Bea,

holding the smoldering remains of the sage bundle. "Your house," she said, "is cleansed."

"Really?" Bea said. "She's gone?"

Amy nodded. "She's gone. If you go to your room, you'll find it several degrees warmer."

"The gum smell's gone, too," Jared said.

The three trouped up the stairs, and Bea was pleasantly surprised. Her room smelled herby, not at all like grape gum, and it was the same temperature as Charlie's room. She had had her doubts, but apparently Amy knew what she was doing.

"Thanks!" Bea said. "You really got her to leave! Fifty bucks, right?"

"That is correct," Amy said.

Bea handed her the money and Amy stuffed it in her tote bag before she and Jared headed out to their car.

———※◯※———

When Mom got home, the first thing she asked was "Why does it smell like Thanksgiving dinner in here?"

"I was burning some incense," Bea said.

"Phew, it must've been strong," Mom said. "And now I have a strange craving for corn-bread dressing."

Bea waited for her mom to notice the salt in the

doorways, or to say something about the house feeling different, but she didn't.

That night, in her newly warm, non-grape–scented room, Bea felt more relaxed than she had since they had moved. She settled down to sleep, thinking calm, soothing thoughts. Peace restored. House cleansed. Problem solved.

CHAPTER 9

Now that Kimmie was gone, Bea could concentrate on spending time with her real friends. She, Olivia, Kayla, and Maeve were truly a team. Yes, they were awesome performing on the dance team together, but it was more than that. They belonged together like a bunch of bananas, or a litter of kittens.

But team membership came with expectations. Like kittens, they were cute, but they had sharp claws.

Bea realized that if she was going to continue to be accepted by the group, she was going to have to sharpen her claws.

The next day, Bea was in the locker room with the rest of the dance team, changing after practice. "Hey," Olivia whispered, "Hannah Thomas is in the bathroom. Go stick this note in her locker before she gets back."

Hannah was one of the sixth-grade girls who had just started on the dance team. She was inexperienced and not as flexible as some of the other girls, so the coach had been putting her in the back row.

Bea looked down at the note, which read, *You dance with the grace of a three-legged cow. Do better, or this will be your only year on dance team.*

Bea winced. "Do you really think this is the best way to critique her dance performance?" she asked. Besides, wasn't it Coach Braden's job to critique dance team members' work?

"People who suck need to know they suck," Olivia said. "Telling them is doing them a favor."

"So why don't you put the note in her locker?" Bea asked.

"Because I'm asking you to do it," Olivia said. "It's for the good of the team."

Bea was being tested, and she didn't like it. But she knew that if she failed the test, she'd like the consequences even less. She would be friendless. She might even become one of the girls who got picked on, like Sophie or Hannah. A person's status could change fast.

She swallowed hard, walked over to Hannah's locker, and stuck the note through the crack in the door. Olivia smiled her approval, and they started changing out of their dance clothes in preparation for a trip to the Mighty Bean.

"Hey, who left this note in my locker?"

Bea felt a prickle of anxiety. She had been hoping they'd be gone by the time Hannah found the note.

Hannah came up to Bea and her friends, waving the note. "Did one of you put this in my locker? Was it you, Olivia?"

Olivia laughed. "Hannah, I promise you I did not put that note in your locker."

Hannah glared at the girls in anger. "Well, somebody better admit it before I take the note to Coach Braden."

Olivia let out a world-weary sigh. "You might as well tell her, Bea."

Oh, Bea thought, *so the test isn't over.* "I was the one who left the note," she said. She was tempted to say that she wasn't the one who had written it, but she knew if she said that, she would fail Olivia's test.

"You?" Hannah said. "You've only been hanging out with their group for a few weeks, and already you're as bad as they are. It's disappointing. I thought you'd be different."

Hannah's words stung, but Bea was determined not to let her feelings show. "Hey, it was constructive criticism," Bea said. "If I danced like a cow, I'd want someone to tell me." As Hannah threw up her hands in exasperation and walked away, Bea heard herself say, "Moo."

"Moo!" Olivia, Kayla, and Maeve echoed, laughing. "Moo!"

"New rule," Olivia said. "Every time Hannah walks by, we moo at her."

Bea laughed along with her friends, but she wasn't having as much fun as she wished she were. *You're as bad as they are*, Hannah had said. Were Olivia and Maeve and Kayla bad? And if they were, did that mean Bea was bad, too?

—∞∘∞—

Bea didn't feel great about what she'd done to Hannah, but the fact that she had passed Olivia's test with flying colors had definitely improved her status in the group. The four girls were inseparable. The next night, they were hanging out in Bea's room, allegedly working on a history project but mostly goofing around on social media.

"Hey, let's look up Hannah Thomas's profile," Olivia said.

"Yeah, let's do it!" Maeve said, laughing.

"I bet she posts all kinds of lame stuff," Kayla said.

Bea typed in Hannah's name and pulled up her page.

"Send her cow pics!" Olivia said, and the other girls whooped with laughter.

Bea pulled up some images of cows and started sending them to Hannah. The more the other girls laughed, the more cow pictures she sent. She didn't think Hannah was cowlike in any way, really, but it felt good to bask in the other girls' approval. "Hey," Bea said, "how about we send her a bunch of messages that just say 'moo'?"

"Do it!" Olivia said, laughing so hard she was crying.

Thirty *moo* messages later, Bea received a message from Hannah. *You guys torture me all the time at school, can't you at least leave me alone when I'm at home?*

"Tell her no," Olivia said. "Tell her that no matter where she is, she's never allowed to forget that she's a dancing cow."

Bea laughed as much as anybody. After her friends had gone home, though, she lay in bed a long time before she could fall asleep. What she had done to Hannah didn't seem so funny anymore. Every time she thought she'd passed her test from Olivia, it seemed there was another one. Were they even really her friends? Or were they just waiting for her to mess up so they could start tormenting her, too?

⸺⊙⊙⸻

Bea awoke with the sensation of pressure on her chest and throat. She couldn't move. Couldn't breathe. She opened her mouth to scream, but a hand clamped over it. She opened her eyes.

She could still make her out, even in the semidarkness. Kimmie was straddling her just like she had straddled Olivia, one hand over her mouth and the other around her throat.

"No screaming," Kimmie said in her little girlish voice. "If you scream, it's all over right now." She took her hand from Bea's mouth.

Bea took several gasps of air before she could finally talk. "You . . . you were gone," she sputtered.

Kimmie laughed. "Stupid girl. I was never gone. I turned up the temperature in your room, quit chewing the gum I like, and stayed invisible. That's all. I could've done that anytime I wanted to."

"But the paranormal investigator—"

"Was a total fake. What, you thought she scared me off with some salt and sage, like I'm supposed to be afraid of *seasonings*?" Kimmie's hands were no longer gripping Bea's throat, but she was still sitting on her, pinning her down so she couldn't move. "The very first conversation we had, Bea, I told you I couldn't leave this house. It's my curse. A few pinches of salt isn't going to change that. The bell ringing was super annoying, though."

Bea remembered how weightless Kimmie used to feel when she would lie with her head on Bea's shoulder. Apparently Kimmie could be heavy when she wanted to.

"You hurt me, you know," Kimmie said. "First you liked that Olivia girl better than me. Then I tried to be an even better best friend, and you didn't even want to be my friend anymore. You preferred a bunch of fake friends to one real one. And you tried to get rid of me."

"I'm sorry," Bea said, her heart feeling like it was going to pound out of her chest. "I didn't mean to hurt you. I . . . I was just afraid of you."

"You should be," Kimmie said, giggling. "You totally should be! You know what? It's probably better that we're not friends. I watched you tonight with those girls. I watched you use your computer to hurt a girl who wasn't even in the room. Those girls that were here tonight—your so-called *friends*— they're bullies. And you're a bully, too, Bea. I thought you were better than them, but you're just the same.

The world would be better without you. I can fix it."

Bea managed to choke out the word "No," but then Kimmie's hands were around her throat so hard that she couldn't form words, couldn't find air.

She hit at Kimmie a few times, but even as she did, she knew it was useless. Kimmie was a girl nobody could hurt anymore. Bea's vision went dark around the edges, and she knew there was nothing she could do. Slowly, she closed her eyes.

CHAPTER 10

As soon as the morning light hit the window, Kimmie stretched her arms out of the covers and got out of bed. She dressed in a pink top, white skinny jeans, and pink canvas slip-on shoes. She brushed her hair and put it in a side ponytail for a change. She brushed on some mascara and some of the pink lipstick, which wasn't nearly shiny enough to suit her.

She didn't need to eat, but she still sat down to break-fast with Mom and Charlie and drank some orange juice and forced down some kind of gritty, grainy muffin. Mom told her that her hair looked cute and different, and she said thank you.

She said goodbye to Mom and Charlie and headed up to the corner to meet Olivia, Kayla, and Maeve so they could walk to school together. They laughed and chattered about the next dance team performance, about the boys they liked, about the girls they hated.

She smiled and laughed and chattered with them, too, even though she knew what kind of girls they were. It was best to do it that way for now. Blend in. Gain their trust.

❦

The real Bea, or what was left of her, looked out the window of the room she couldn't leave. No one could see her, but she could see all the way to the corner. She saw Olivia and Kayla and Maeve, talking and laughing. She saw the one wearing her hair, her clothes, and her skin, talking and laughing, too. She knew that Olivia and Kayla and Maeve were deeply flawed, but looking at them right now, they seemed innocent. They were innocent because they didn't know that the thing occupying Bea's skin was not Bea herself but something that existed only to seek revenge against girls like them. They didn't know enough to be afraid, but Bea knew. She was afraid for them.

But there was nothing she could do to help them now.

94

CHAPTER 1

By three o'clock, it was obvious that Casey's dad wasn't going to show up.

The plan had been for him to pick up Casey at one p.m. and take him to the zoo. They were going to buy hot dogs and ice cream and walk around to look at the animals. At two-thirty p.m., they were going to head to the amphitheater for Casey's favorite thing, the bird show, and watch the zoo's collection of parrots and raptors perform "stunning feats of avian intelligence," as the animal trainer who hosted the program always said.

But the bird show had already been going on for half an hour, and the zoo closed at four-thirty p.m. And there Casey sat on the couch in his and his mom's small apartment, once again waiting for a father who was absent more than he was present.

"Disappointed again?" his mom said, sitting down on the couch beside him.

Casey nodded.

His mom was already dressed in her "business casual" button-down shirt and khakis. She was working the five-till-midnight shift at the call center tonight. It was a job with weird hours, but it worked with her class schedule at the community college. "I've texted him a dozen times, but I haven't heard a peep," she said. "He's probably let his phone run out of charge."

"Or didn't pay the bill," Casey said. His dad was terrible with money. Mom didn't complain about it to Casey, but he had heard her a few times on the phone with friends talking about his dad's failure to pay his child support.

"Yeah, that's even more likely," Mom said, ruffling Casey's hair. "I'm sorry, kiddo. I know you were looking forward to going to the zoo."

"I should've known better than to look forward to it," Casey said. "Dad only comes through half the time at most."

"I could've definitely done some smarter shopping all those years ago when I went to the Husband Store," Mom said, with a sad little laugh. "Instead, I just said

'That one's cute' and grabbed the first one I saw. *But* he did give me you, so that was a good thing." She stood up. "Hey, why don't I run across the street and get you a pizza before I have to go to work? I have a coupon for a five-dollar large with your name on it."

"Sure, Mom. Thanks." A pizza wasn't much compared to a trip to the zoo, but he knew Mom wanted to help him feel better, and a five-dollar pizza was what she could afford.

Back when Casey's parents had still been married, they had lived in a spacious three-bedroom house in the suburbs. Casey's room had been huge compared to the room he had now, and they had had a good-sized yard with a tree house his dad had built when Casey was little. But even though the house was bigger and more comfortable than the apartment where Casey and his mom now lived, it hadn't been a very happy place.

Casey's mom and dad had argued all the time. Sometimes it was about who was responsible for what or Casey's dad failing to do what he had promised. But more often it was over money. His mom would mention some bill that had gone unpaid, and then there would be raised voices and slamming doors and eventually Casey's dad storming out of the house, starting the car, backing out of the driveway too fast, and speeding down the road.

One night about a year ago, he sped away and didn't come back. Mom and Casey moved into their apartment once their house was sold, and Casey's dad moved into a smaller apartment of his own.

Living with just his mom was calmer. Money was tight, but the apartment complex was still in Casey's old school district so he was able to go to eighth grade with all his friends. He was in walking distance of the public library, where he could check out the zoology books he loved, and he had his old but still functional laptop for reading about weird animals and watching animal videos. He did wish his mom weren't so busy and tired all the time, but he was also proud of her for going back to college and working so hard to support them.

Casey's mom brought home the cheese pizza and gave Casey a peck on the cheek before she left for work. He got a soda from the fridge and sat down on the couch with the pizza box on his lap. He turned on the Animal Channel, which was showing a documentary about orangutans (he loved orangutans—their soulful eyes and their domed heads with silly orange hair that looked like a comb-over gone wrong). He watched the orangutans swing through the trees and gobbled up half of the large pizza.

His appetite was enormous these days. A shrew

needed to consume two hundred to three hundred percent of its body weight every day to survive. Since Casey had turned thirteen, he had been eating like a shrew.

Once the orangutan documentary was over, he put the pizza box in the fridge and his empty glass in the sink. It was time to feed his pets.

Casey didn't have all the pets he wanted. His dad had always claimed he had allergies and had forbidden dogs and cats when they were living in the house, and now that it was just Casey and his mom, the apartment was too small for a menagerie. Plus, pet care cost money. His mom had agreed to some small "tank pets," though, and Casey loved them.

"Hi, guys," he said as he walked into his room. "Ready for some dinner?"

He leaned over the mini aquarium that held two African dwarf frogs, which were tinier than goldfish. He had named them Jekyll and Hyde, but to be honest, they were identical, so he couldn't tell which one was which. He shook their food onto the surface of the water, and they paddled up to get it, their little mouths opening and closing over the crumbs.

Once the frogs were taken care of, Casey went over to the large tank beside his bed. The tank's inhabitants, two brown-and-white fancy rats named Igor and

Renfield, scrabbled over to their food bowl and looked up at him, their little pink noses twitching. Casey knew that to them, his presence meant their two favorite things: food and attention. It was nice to be appreciated for something so simple.

"You guys know what's coming, don't you?" Casey poured a small handful of food into their bowl, and the two rodents happily started to chow down. "Cuddles and playtime after dinner, okay?" he said.

Casey had gotten Igor and Renfield when they were just babies, and while he knew some people found rats gross, they weren't gross at all. They were friendly and social and loved to play on their exercise wheel and in the network of tunnels he had set up in their habitat. They liked to be held and cuddled. True, they pooped a lot, but Casey didn't mind cleaning their tank once a week and changing out the wood shavings. It was part of being a responsible pet owner.

But one thing about the rats made him sad. He knew that, unlike larger pets, they wouldn't live long. Two to three years, max. He was so attached to Igor and Renfield that he couldn't even think about the day in the not-distant future when he would have to say goodbye.

In Casey's opinion, the ideal pet, in addition to

being intelligent and affectionate, would have a long life-span, so it could be a real companion through the years. This was why Casey's dream pet wasn't a cat or a dog, but an African grey parrot. The bird show was his favorite thing at the zoo because of Albert the African grey, who could perform a wide range of animal noises, sound effects, and snippets from songs. How cool would it be to have a pet you could train to have a conversation with you? And African greys lived as long as sixty years, so they could be in a family for generations.

But birds that can live for so long and learn so much were expensive. When he'd looked online, Casey had found young African grey parrots for around a thousand dollars—way out of his mom's price range. Most months, she made just enough to cover the rent and groceries, so there was no way she could pay so much for a bird.

Casey was just about to take the rats out for playtime when the doorbell rang. It was an odd time for a visitor, so he looked through the peephole to make sure it wasn't a stranger.

It was his dad. And he was seven hours late.

Casey seriously thought about not letting him in, but then he relented and unchained the door.

There was something boyish about Casey's dad.

His dark brown hair was always flopping in his eyes, and he was prone to gestures like shrugging and shoving his hands into his pockets. He called everyone "dude," regardless of their gender or age.

"Dude!" he said, as Casey had known he would, holding up his hand for a high five.

Casey gave him a half-hearted hand slap. "Dad, you're super late."

"I know, I know." He hung his head as if embarrassed, though truthfully, he didn't seem that upset. "I got to watching the game. A couple of the guys dropped by, and I kinda lost track of time. You should've seen the touchdown we made. It was awesome!"

Casey thought it was weird how his dad always referred to football games as if he himself were on the team. "We were supposed to go to the zoo," Casey reminded him.

Dad sat down on the couch. "Aren't you getting kind of old for the zoo?"

Casey thought about saying *Aren't you getting kind of old for football?* but he didn't. "I don't go to the zoo like a little kid goes to the zoo," Casey said. "I want to be a vet for exotic animals when I grow up. I go there to learn, not for the petting zoo."

"I know, dude," his dad said, propping his feet up on the coffee table, a habit Casey's mom hated. "It's just that . . . by the time I was your age, I was living and breathing sports."

"Well, I'm not you," Casey said, because really, what else was there to say?

Casey knew he would be less of a disappointment to his dad if he were an athlete. Maybe if he were the kind of kid who loved to throw a ball back and forth, his dad would show up more to spend time with him. But sports bored Casey, and he wasn't good at faking enthusiasm for things that bored him. He figured this was one trait he and his dad had in common, anyway. His dad couldn't really fake enthusiasm for the short, glasses-wearing nerdy teenager he had ended up with instead of the athletic son of his dreams.

"Yeah, I'm not sure how I got such a geek for a kid," his dad said. "It's cool, though. Takes all kinds. Hey . . . I was thinking we might go out and grab a burger or something."

"I already ate. Mom got me a pizza before she left for work."

"Got any left?" Dad asked. "I'm starving."

"Sure. Hang on." Casey went into the kitchen and got the pizza box from the fridge. He poured his dad a glass of fruit punch and grabbed some napkins. This is how it was with Dad. On the rare occasions when he did show up, Casey would end up taking care of him instead of the other way around.

"Awesome," Dad said when Casey came in with the pizza and punch. He set the pizza box and drink on the coffee table and grabbed the remote. "You mind if I check the sports scores?"

"Knock yourself out," Casey said.

Casey's dad watched sports scores, and Casey watched his dad finish the pizza. It was kind of a shame. He had been looking forward to having cold pizza for breakfast. But it was typical of his dad to take away something else that Casey had been looking forward to.

Full of pizza, Casey's dad was soon snoring in front of the TV. Casey left him and went to his room to play with Igor and Renfield and to see if there were any good new animal videos on YouTube. He settled in with his laptop and didn't look up until his phone buzzed with a text from his mom saying, *Leaving work. Home in 15 min.*

Casey had forgotten his dad was even there! He put the rats back in their habitat, ran into the living room, and shook his dad's shoulder.

"Huh?" he said, opening one eye.

"Time to go. Mom's on her way home from work, and she's not going to be too happy about you being here asleep on her couch."

"Hey, this couch used to be in our house—it should

be *our* couch. But I guess your mom got custody of it, too." He yawned and stretched. "Yeah, I'd better scoot. Don't want the dragon lady to breathe her fire on me. Thanks for the warning, dude."

"Sure." Casey didn't like hearing his mom described as a dragon lady, but the less he argued, the more quickly he could get his dad out of the apartment.

His dad was on his feet and headed toward the door. "So we'll hang out again next weekend, just us guys, okay?"

"Okay, Dad," Casey said. Though he didn't feel like the two of them had really hung out together at all.

CHAPTER 2

Sometimes when he was procrastinating doing homework, Casey would look at the "Pets" section of online classified ads, just to see what kind of animals were available. There were always ads for kittens and guinea pigs and weird breed mixes of dogs: Maltipoos and Chiweenies, and once, a pit bull–corgi mix that looked like it had had its legs swapped with another dog's. Today, though, there was one ad that made his heart pound fast:

Free to a good home. African grey parrot, age unknown. Smart, friendly. Cage included. I am elderly and my health problems no longer allow me to care for this bird. You may have him for free if you prove to me that you can provide a safe, loving home.

Casey jumped up from his seat and ran to find his mom. She was sitting at the kitchen table doing her own homework, frowning in concentration. She looked up at him. "I tell you what, this math stuff really leaves you if you haven't done it in several years. Especially if you weren't that good at it in the first place."

There was only one thing that Casey wanted to talk about, and it certainly wasn't math. "Mom, there's an ad online for an African grey parrot that's free to a good home."

Mom raised an eyebrow. "There are lots of ads online for a lot of things, and many of them are scams."

"Yeah, this didn't seem like a scam, though. It was some old person who said they were sick and couldn't take care of their bird anymore."

"Huh," his mom said. "Email me the link, and I'll take a look at it later. If it seems legit, I'll give them a call tomorrow."

Casey couldn't stop grinning. "Really? If it's legit, you'd let me have the bird?"

"I'm not making any promises," his mom said. "But I am willing to discuss the possibility."

He felt himself fill with hope as if he were inflating like a balloon. "Thanks, Mom!"

It was hard for Casey to concentrate in school the next day, because he kept thinking about the parrot. Was there a catch somehow? Was there some hidden way the man was asking for money? Was the bird sick or defective? Or was this just as it seemed to be, a dream come true?

"Casey. Casey? Anybody home?" Ari, Casey's best friend said.

Casey pulled himself away from staring out the window of the bus. "Sorry, what?"

"You've been a million miles away all day today," said Ari.

"I know. I'm sorry. It's just . . . there may be something big that's going to happen to me, but I don't know yet if it's gonna happen or not."

"Wow," Ari said. "That's really vague."

"I know. I'm afraid to tell you what it is because I don't want to jinx it."

Ari grinned, showing the gap between his two front teeth. "If I guess and get it right, will you tell me?"

Casey laughed. What were the chances that Ari would actually guess? "Sure."

Ari knitted his brow like he was thinking hard. "Your family may have won the lottery."

Casey shook his head. "Mom doesn't believe in buying lottery tickets. And if Dad won, he wouldn't give any of the money to us, so it wouldn't matter."

"Okay, okay, I'm just getting warmed up here." He stroked his chin thoughtfully. "You may be getting a car."

"I'm thirteen. What would I do with a car?"

"You may be getting a car . . . with a chauffeur?"

Casey smiled. "Not even close."

"Wait, it's an animal, isn't it? You love animals!" Ari said. "You're getting a dog!"

"Nope, but you're getting warmer." Casey had never told anybody outside his family about wanting an African grey parrot. It had always seemed so far out of the realm of possibility that talking about it was pointless, as if he were saying he wanted a million dollars. Of course he wanted something he couldn't have. Who didn't?

"Okay, so it's a pet," Ari said. "An iguana? A ferret? A coatimundi?"

Casey laughed, trying to imagine what it would be

like to have a coatimundi as a house pet. "You're a good friend, but you're a terrible guesser."

As soon as Casey walked into the apartment, his mom looked up from her textbook and said, "Yes, I talked to the guy with the parrot."

"Hey, you answered before I even asked."

His mom ruffled his hair. "What can I say? I'm psychic." She took the pitcher of fruit punch from the fridge and poured Casey a glass. "Mr. Byron is his name—the man, not the parrot. He seems like a nice older guy, and he invited us to come to his house to meet the bird. I'm squeamish about going to strangers' houses, so I asked if we could meet somewhere public. We're meeting in the public library parking lot at six o'clock. He used to work in the library, he said."

Now Casey felt like his heart was not just inflating like a balloon but floating like one. "And he's bringing the bird?"

His mom smiled. "He is. It likes car rides, apparently."

Mr. Byron arrived in the library parking lot in an ancient, once-white Volvo. He was bald on top with long gray hair stringing down the sides of his head. When he got out of the car, he displayed an impressive potbelly pushing against his flannel shirt. He reminded Casey of Benjamin Franklin.

"Ms. Matthews?" he said to Casey's mom.

"Laura," she said, holding out her hand to shake. "And this is Casey, my resident zoologist I was telling you about."

"Casey," Mr. Byron said. Casey could tell that Mr. Byron was one of those adults who was strangely formal when talking to kids, as if excess politeness would hide the fact that he wasn't sure what to say to them. "Well, I believe there's someone you both want to meet. Let me get him."

He opened the car's back door and leaned into the back seat for a few moments. When he stood up and turned around, a stunning, medium-sized African grey parrot was perched on his arm. "This is Dorian Grey," Mr. Byron said. "But I call him Dodie for short."

"Dorian Grey," Casey's mom said, laughing. "Very clever."

Casey couldn't believe how beautiful the parrot was. His bill was black, his feathers scalloped and silver. His intense golden eyes, surrounded by white feathers, focused on Casey with curiosity. His tail feathers were a vivid scarlet.

"He's perfect," Casey said.

"I've got a leash around his ankle so he can't fly away," Mr. Byron said. "Some people clip their birds' wings, but that always struck me as cruel. Birds should be able to fly. And sing." He stroked the bird's chest. "Sing them a song, Dodie."

"Oh, Polly, pretty Polly, come go along with me . . ." The bird's voice was gravelly, but he could carry a tune surprisingly well. He looked right at Casey as he sang.

"Before Dodie came to me, he lived with an elderly lady in Kentucky," Mr. Byron said. "He knows all these bits of old Appalachian folk songs. 'Pretty Polly' is the one he sings the most, I think because the lady called him that." Mr. Byron smiled at Casey and his mom. "But I couldn't bear to keep the name Polly. Too unoriginal."

"Unlike Dorian Grey, which is perfect," Casey's mom said. She turned to Casey. "*The Picture of Dorian Gray* is a novel by Oscar Wilde about a man who lives forever but never shows any signs of aging. The twist is that he has a portrait of himself that ages instead."

"A very good summary," Mr. Byron said, nodding his approval.

Casey's mom looked a little embarrassed. "I'm an English major," she said.

"So was I!" Mr. Byron stroked the bird's head. "And I figure this fellow will live a long time and still look fabulous. Plus, he's gray, and I never met a pun I didn't like." He looked at Casey. "So your mom tells me you'd be Dodie's primary caretaker and that you know a lot about animals."

"Yes, sir. I study animals all the time. I want to go to college to be a vet." Casey was excited and nervous. Now that he had met Dodie, he couldn't imagine living without him. But what if Mr. Byron decided that he wasn't responsible enough to be a good bird owner?

"Well, let's see if Dodie takes to you." Mr. Byron stepped closer to Casey. "Hold out your arm, and let's see if Dodie will come to you."

Nervously, Casey held his arm out in the same position as Mr. Byron's, close enough that Dodie could step onto it if he chose to. Dodie looked intensely into Casey's eyes, then extended his leg and held one foot out in the air as if he were still deciding what to do. Finally, he stepped onto Casey's arm, first one clawed foot, then the other. Casey held on to the end of the bird's leash to make sure he was secure.

"Well, look at that!" Mr. Byron said. "He doesn't do that with just anybody."

"I feel honored," Casey said, smiling. He felt like instead of choosing a pet, a pet was choosing him.

"And you should." Mr. Byron looked at Casey, then his mother. "Now, a parrot isn't a pet you can be casual about. It's a real commitment. Dodie needs a lot more than just food and water. He needs affection but also stimulation. He's smart—smarter than some people I've met—and if you don't talk to him and provide him with a variety of activities, he'll get bored and anxious and destructive. And a sad birdie is— what, Dodie?"

"A sad birdie is a bad birdie!" Dodie squawked.

Casey and his mom laughed.

"And you definitely don't want a bad birdie," Mr. Byron said. His tone was light, but Casey could tell he meant business.

"I'll make sure he has plenty of conversation and plenty of activities to keep him busy," Casey said. Dodie took a few steps up Casey's arm. "That tickles," he said, laughing. Soon Dodie was sitting on Casey's shoulder, nuzzling his hair.

"Oh, that's a sign he really likes you!" Mr. Byron said. "We call that 'playing pirate.'"

"Pieces of eight! Pieces of eight!" Dodie squawked. It was a line Casey thought he might have heard in a movie once.

"That's what the parrot says in *Treasure Island*, isn't it?" Casey's mom asked.

Mr. Byron nodded. "English major."

Mr. Byron watched Dodie nuzzle Casey. "Well, I think this is a match made in birdie heaven. If you want to take him, you can have him."

"Really?" Casey felt tears welling in his eyes. He had never cried from happiness before.

"Really. If it's okay with your mom."

Casey's mom nodded. "It's okay with me. Are you sure that you don't want to charge us anything, though? I mean, when Casey told me about the ad, I couldn't believe you were giving an African grey away for free."

"There are more important things than money. Just because somebody pays me doesn't mean they'd take good care of Dodie. It was more important to find a good match for him in terms of personality, and I think I've found that."

Casey smiled as the bird rubbed his cheek against his. "If you don't mind my asking, sir, why do you want to part with him?"

Mr. Byron didn't meet Casey's eyes, perhaps because he feared becoming too emotional. "Well, like I said, keeping a bird is a big commitment, and at my age, it's more of a commitment than I can handle. Dodie will be better off in younger hands."

"Well, I'll take good care of him," Casey said. "The very best care."

"I know you will," Mr. Byron said. "And if you take good care of Dodie, he'll take good care of you."

Dodie sat on Casey's shoulder on the ride home. "Thanks for letting me have him, Mom," he said.

"You're welcome. I'm glad you can have something that you've wanted for so long." Mom stopped for a red light and turned her head to smile at Casey and his new pet. "Plus, the price was certainly right."

Casey stroked Dodie's soft feathers. "This has made me happier than anything I can remember in a long time."

"I'm glad," Mom said as they pulled into the apartment complex. "You've had a lot of changes in your life lately, and not all of them good. I'm happy to do something to make you happy."

Casey brought Dodie's cage into his room. Mr. Byron had written a long note outlining Dodie's daily care, and Casey read it carefully and set up Dodie's habitat according to Mr. Byron's specifications. He lined the bottom of the bird cage with fresh paper towels. He put in the red rubber ring Mr. Byron had called Dodie's "chewy toy" and the tube of blue fuzzy fabric Mr. Byron had said was his "snuggly toy." He filled his water dish and poured his food dish full of the parrot pellets Mr. Byron had provided. "Welcome home," Casey said, helping Dodie step into his cage.

"Home," Dodie said, settling on his perch and starting to swing.

CHAPTER 3

Every day when Casey got home from school, he would go straight to Dodie's cage. "I'm home!" Casey would say, and Dodie would flap his wings and squawk, "Hello! Hello!"

Casey had to admit it was nice for a creature to be that happy to see you.

Today, they were working on some tricks Casey had seen a trainer doing with her parrot on a YouTube video. Casey did a circular motion with his hand over Dodie's head and said, "Spin."

Dodie spun around like a birdie ballerina.

"Good boy!" Casey gave Dodie a sunflower seed.

Next they worked on "wave hello." Almost immediately, Dodie lifted his right foot and wiggled it.

"Good boy!" Casey dispensed another sunflower seed.

"Kiss," Dodie said.

"What?" Casey hadn't taught him that.

"Kiss," Dodie repeated.

"Okay." Casey moved his face close to Dodie's, and Dodie touched his beak to Casey's lips.

"Hey, you taught *me* a trick," Casey said, laughing. "Maybe you should give me a sunflower seed."

Casey had read about African greys and watched lots of videos of them, but he was still shocked and amazed by how smart Dodie was. Any trick he showed him, any words he said to him, Dodie repeated them right away. He wondered if Dodie was extra smart even by the standards of his breed's high intelligence level.

"Sing me a song, Dodie," Casey said.

"Oh, Polly, pretty Polly, come go along with me / Before we get married some pleasures to see." His voice was high and mournful like some mountain man playing his banjo and singing on his front porch.

Casey gave him another sunflower seed.

The front door opened.

"Hi, Mom!" Casey called.

"Hi, Mom!" Dodie repeated.

Mom laughed. "Hi, boys! Let me get changed out

of these stupid work clothes, and I'll get dinner started."

Casey took Dodie to the kitchen, sat at the table, and got out his homework while Mom chopped up vegetables for stir-fry. Dodie sat on Casey's shoulder and nuzzled his hair, but then flew from his perch on Casey to the kitchen counter.

"Hi, Dodie," Mom said. "Don't poop on the counter, okay?"

Casey watched as Dodie cocked his head at her. "Whatcha doin'?" Dodie asked.

"Um . . . cooking dinner," Mom answered as if she were a little nervous about being interrogated by a parrot.

"Yummy!" Dodie squawked.

Mom laughed and gave him a slice of carrot. "You know," she said, "I've always been under the impression that parrots just repeat what they're told, but that was like an actual *conversation*."

"I know," Casey said. "He's crazy smart."

She looked at Dodie with fascination. "I mean, he asked me a question, and when I answered, he responded to my answer. Are parrots supposed to be able to do that?"

"I don't know if they're supposed to be able to, but I know that Dodie does. And I can't teach him tricks fast enough."

"Wow," Mom said, offering another carrot slice to

Dodie. "It's almost like having something more than a pet. He reminds me of a really intelligent toddler. A weird, feathery, squawking toddler."

"A weird, feathery, squawking toddler that poops a lot," Casey said.

"Well, toddlers poop a lot, too," his mom said, grinning. "But it's interesting to have him around. I'm glad we got him."

"Me too."

"I love you, Mom," Dodie squawked.

"I love you, too, Dodie," Mom said. "Here, try some broccoli."

After dinner, Casey put Dodie back in his cage so he could take out the rats for cuddle and playtime. He had been trying hard to make sure Renfield and Igor didn't feel ignored because of the new addition to his menagerie.

"Hey, guys, ready for cuddles?" Casey lifted the rats out of their habitat and sat down on the floor with them. They crawled all over his lap and licked at his hands. "Are you being lovey, or are you just looking for treats?" Casey asked, giving each of them a rub behind their ears. Rats loved to be rubbed behind their ears for some reason.

A clacking sound came from Dodie's cage. Casey looked up to see Dodie, his neck craned, his wings spread. The clacking sound was coming from his bill. The pupils of his eyes contracted to pinpoints, expanded, then contracted again. Casey knew from his reading that these were the behaviors of an angry bird.

"Buddy, what's wrong?" Casey asked. "You're acting all jealous."

Dodie flashed his eyes and clacked his bill again.

"My little rat buddies have to get some attention, too," Casey said.

Dodie hissed like an angry cat.

"Okay, well, you're just going to have to sulk for a few minutes." Casey turned his back on Dodie. "These little guys need love, too."

Once the rats had had half an hour of playtime, he stood up and put them back in their tank. He walked over to the birdcage where Dodie was sitting on his perch, his wings closed tight against his body.

"There's no need for you to be jealous," Casey said. "You're my birdie, and I'm your boy."

Dodie held out his foot.

"Okay, you can come out for a few minutes." He held out his arm for Dodie to perch on it.

The doorbell rang.

"Ding dong! Ding dong!" Dodie squawked.

Casey laughed. "Okay, let's go see who's at the door."

Casey's mom had already let Ari in. He lived in the apartment complex across the street, so he dropped by frequently. Ari was holding his skateboard. Whenever he wasn't in school, he was either riding his skateboard or carrying it. It was like an extension of his body.

"Hey," Ari said. "I thought I'd stop by and see your—" He looked at Casey's shoulder and grinned— "There he is!"

"Yep, this is Dodie," Casey said. "Sit down, and maybe you two can get acquainted."

Ari sat on the couch, and Casey sat beside him. Dodie walked down Casey's shoulder and perched on his forearm. "If you hold your arm out, too, he might come sit on you." Ari held out his arm, and Casey said, "Dodie, this is Ari. Ari is my friend."

Dodie stepped from Casey's arm to Ari's. He tilted his head, looked at Ari, and said, "Friend."

Ari's eyes widened. "Whoa! Has he ever said that before?"

"Not where I could hear him," Casey said. "He's picking up new things all the time."

"Wow, Dodie," Ari said. "You make my cat look stupid."

"Stupid cat! Stupid cat!" Dodie squawked, then followed up with a series of highly realistic meows.

Both boys laughed.

"Can you imagine him meowing like that at your cat?" Casey said. "It would drive her crazy!"

"It would," Ari said, laughing some more. "Hey, Dodie, I have an idea. Would you like to be a skater boy?"

He set down his skateboard and held Dodie so he could step onto it. Once Dodie had both feet on the board, Ari pushed it gently across the floor. "Whee!" Dodie squawked. "Again! Again!"

"This is awesome," Ari said. "I've got to film it." He took out his phone and aimed it at Dodie.

Dodie shrieked and beat his wings. "No no no no no!" he squawked.

"Camera shy, huh?" Ari said. "Sorry, dude. I'll put it away."

Dodie calmed down as soon as the phone was out of sight, and Casey and Ari took turns giving him skateboard rides. Ari made up a song called "Skater Bird" to the tune of "Surfin' Bird," and Dodie bobbed his head as Ari sang.

After Ari left, Casey put Dodie back in the cage so he could finish his homework and take a shower before bed. After he'd brushed his teeth and put on his pajamas, he did his nighttime ritual of telling all his animals good night. It was like that book his mom used to read to him when he was little, where the bunny said good night to all the things in his room.

He peeked into the aquarium. "Good night, my frogs."

He peeked into the rodent habitat. "Good night, my rats."

He stood beside the bird cage. Dodie's eyes were already closed. "Good night, my birdie."

Dodie's eyes opened. "Good night, my boy," he squawked.

CHAPTER 4

Casey and Ari were sitting together on the school bus. "I know we've got to work on our project when we get to your house," Ari said, "but can we play with your bird, too?"

Casey smiled. "Dude, you are *obsessed* with Dodie."

"He's so cool, though! I've never spent time around an animal that smart before."

"We'll definitely play with him," Casey said. "As a matter of fact, if we don't play with him for a while first, he won't let us get anything done."

Dodie was establishing himself not just as a creature of habit, but as a creature with strong opinions and preferences. He liked his fruits and vegetables diced extra small. He liked to have his head and chest stroked but did not like his back to be touched. He liked TV, especially animal shows and cooking shows. He liked classic rock but not heavy metal. He ignored the frogs but hated the rats and always went into a snit when Casey paid attention to them.

When Casey unlocked the apartment door, he could hear Dodie screeching in his cage. Ari looked concerned, but Casey said, "He always does that when somebody opens the door. He's better than an alarm system."

"Or a watch dog," Ari said.

"I'm home," Casey called.

"Hello, hello," Dodie squawked back at him.

They went into Casey's room, which, Casey had to admit, he sometimes thought of as Dodie's room. "My birdie!" Casey said as soon as he made eye contact with Dodie.

"My boy!" Dodie said.

"He sounds so happy to see you," Ari said. "My cat doesn't even wake up when I come home."

Casey opened Dodie's cage and let Dodie step onto his arm. "I brought Ari home with me today. You remember Ari." Casey actually had no idea if Dodie remembered Ari or not, but he was in the habit of talking to Dodie like a person. "Ari's my friend."

"Boyfriend!" Dodie squawked.

Ari laughed. "I'm your boy's friend, but I'm not his boyfriend."

"Boyfriend!" Dodie repeated.

"I'm pretty sure that distinction is lost on him," Casey said. He set Dodie down on his dresser. "Why don't we show Ari your new trick?" He got out the necessary handful of sunflower seeds, then set out a plastic cup he had cut in half vertically so it made an arch. He got out a ball, the small bouncing kind you could sometimes buy out of gum machines. "Okay, Dodie, wanna play soccer?"

He set the ball down in front of Dodie. "Play soccer, Dodie." Dodie kicked the ball with a gnarled, clawed foot. The ball rolled straight into the "goal" Casey had made out of the plastic cup. "Good birdie!" Casey said, feeding Dodie a sunflower seed. "Now what do you say when you win at soccer?"

"GOOOAAAALLL!" Dodie yelled just like an overdramatic soccer announcer.

Ari laughed and applauded. "That was awesome! You've got to get over being camera shy, Dodie. You could be a star." He walked over to the rats' habitat. Renfield was really going to town on the exercise wheel, while Igor was drinking out of the water bottle. "And how are the rats today?" Ari asked.

"Stinky. Loud," Dodie said.

Ari looked at Dodie, then at Casey, with an astonished look on his face.

"He doesn't like the rats," Casey said.

"I hear that. Casey, has it ever occurred to you that Dodie might be . . . you know—"

"Way smarter than even other African grey parrots? Yeah. I think he's definitely at the top of his class."

Ari nodded. "Total birdie valedictorian."

Casey didn't want to talk about Dodie's intelligence because while it fascinated him, it also freaked him out a little. "Why don't we get a snack before we start on our homework?"

"Snack! Snack!" Dodie squawked.

"He doesn't like the rats, but he does like snacks," Casey said, smiling. He held out his arm for Dodie to hop on. "Come on, let's go to the kitchen."

Casey poured a glass of fruit punch for Ari and one for himself. He got a box of cheesy crackers from the pantry and poured some in a bowl. He took a bunch of grapes from the fridge and plucked a few and cut them up for Dodie. The three of them sat at the kitchen table, munching on cheesy crackers and grapes. Casey looked at Ari, then at Dodie and felt strangely happy. *My two best friends*, he thought.

When Casey's mom came home, Casey and Ari were working on their social studies project at the kitchen table. Dodie was "playing pirate" on Casey's shoulder.

"Hey, boys," Casey's mom said, hanging up her jacket and her purse on the hook by the door.

"Hi, Mom," Casey said.

"Hi, Ms. Laura," Ari said.

"Hi, Mom," Dodie said.

Ari laughed. "Ms. Laura, I had no idea that you were Dodie's mom, too."

Laura laughed along with him. "Yep. I sure am. I got really bored sitting on the egg all that time, waiting for it to hatch." She stepped out of her dress shoes. "Ari, if it's okay with your mom, you're welcome to stay for dinner. It's nothing fancy. I'm just going to throw together some tacos."

"Tacos sound great. Thanks!" Ari said.

Casey felt very cozy and homey, sitting at the table with Ari and Dodie, working on their project while Mom cooked dinner, humming to herself. Sometimes Dodie would join in on the humming. There were days when Casey wished he could have a roomy house again and enough money for a decent allowance and two parents who lived with him. But on nights like tonight, he felt like what he had was just right.

Casey came home from school in a good mood. He had gotten an A on the research paper he wrote about parrots, and he had gotten a B minus on his math test, which, for him, was a cause for celebration. Dodie was emitting joyful squawks from his room.

"How's my birdie?" Casey asked as soon as he got to his room and set down his backpack.

"How's my boy?" Dodie asked.

"Good. I'll get you out in just a sec, okay?" He peeked into the aquarium. "How are my froggies?" They didn't answer, but they were alive, which was all he asked of his aquatic pets.

"And how are my rats?" Casey peeked into the tank. He looked in the tunnels and the little house where they liked to hide, but he didn't see them. He took the lid off the habitat and dug around in the wood shavings in case they had dug under and buried themselves. They were gone. "Igor? Renfield?" he called, as if one of them might answer him. He felt a rush of panic, tinged with sadness. "I don't understand! Where are my rats?"

"Good riddance to bad rubbish," Dodie said.

CHAPTER 5

"D o you think we could put up signs around the apartment complex?" Casey asked, still sniffling. He had been crying more than he would ever let anybody besides his mom see.

"We can," Mom said. "But being realistic, rats are really good at hiding when they don't want to be seen. Also, even if somebody did see them, they might be squeamish about picking them up."

"Which is stupid," Casey said.

"It is," his mom agreed. "But 'human' and 'stupid' aren't exactly mutually exclusive."

"They still could be somewhere in the apartment," Casey said, trying to remain hopeful, even though it felt like they'd looked everywhere: under both beds, under every piece of furniture, and in every cabinet and closet.

"They could. And that's why I thought you were so smart to put their habitat on the floor with the cover off and make a little ramp they can climb to get back in. Once they get too hungry or thirsty, their habitat is going to start sounding pretty comfy."

Casey sighed. "I hope so. What I don't understand is how they got out. I know I left the lid on."

"Yeah, but the lid has a place on the screen that's a little torn. It looks too small for them to have gotten through, but rodents can be quite the escape artists."

"They never tried to escape before," Casey said. His worst fear about this situation popped into his mind. "I wonder—" he said, but then cut himself off.

"What?" his mom said, putting a comforting hand on his shoulder.

"I wonder," he said, barely above a whisper, "if Dodie had something to do with it. He hates the rats."

"What could he have done with just a beak and claws to work with?"

"I don't know, but when I played with the rats instead of him, he always got really jealous. Plus, he thought they were noisy and smelled."

Mom knitted her brow. "Casey? Do you know what anthropomorphism is?"

"Anthropo—what?" Since his mom had gone back to college, she was always throwing around a lot of big words.

"It's when we give human qualities to animals, like in the stories you liked as a little kid where animals wear clothes and talk."

"Oh-kay?" Casey didn't know what she was getting at.

"I think it's important that we don't ascribe too many human qualities to Dodie. I mean, I know he sounds like a human sometimes, and he can string together a lot of commands, but he's still a bird. A smart bird, but just a bird."

"So you don't think he could've done anything to Igor and Renfield?" Just saying their names was painful.

"No, because Dodie isn't some kind of criminal mastermind. He can't *plot*. The rats got out on their own. Animals are not like us. They're not rational."

"Okay." Casey wanted to believe her. He really did. But then he kept thinking of Dodie's words: *Good riddance to bad rubbish.* "What if we can't find them?"

"Even if we can't find them, they'll be okay," his mom said, giving his hand a squeeze. "They'll find food and they'll survive. It's what rats have done for centuries. As a species, they'll probably outlast humans."

Casey nodded, too sad to speak. He loved the rats, and when he played with them, he liked to think they loved him, too. He wondered if his mom would think that thought was also anthropomorphism.

Mom made grilled cheese sandwiches and tomato soup for dinner, a combination Casey usually found comforting, but tonight he didn't have much of an appetite and gave up after a couple bites. Dodie was perched on the back of one of the kitchen chairs, letting Casey feed him grapes.

"I'm sorry this is kind of a skimpy meal," Mom said, dipping the corner of her grilled cheese into her soup. "Things are going to be a little tight till I get paid on Friday."

Casey and his mom never went hungry, but toward the end of the month, they tended to eat less-expensive food: boxed macaroni and cheese, canned soups, pancakes. "I don't guess Dad has paid the child support?" Casey said.

"What do you think?" Mom's tone was bitter. "Oh, I'm sorry, honey. I try not to talk badly about him in front of you. I don't want to put you in the middle of our adult conflicts."

"It's okay," Casey said, idly stirring his soup with his spoon. "I know Dad isn't very responsible."

"That's putting it mildly," Mom said. "If there's a

good choice and a bad choice to make, he'll always make the bad one. That's why he never has any money." She took out her phone. "I've been texting him about his payment all day and haven't heard a peep."

"You can't get blood from a turnip!" Dodie squawked.

Mom gave Dodie a strange look but went back to texting. "Where did he get all these homespun expressions?" she said.

And why do they always relate so directly to what people are talking about? Casey wondered, feeding Dodie another grape.

After dinner, Casey put Dodie back in his cage so he could look for the rats again. "I'm going to put you in here for just a little bit, then you can come out and play again."

"I love you, my boy."

Casey sniffed. He really did love Dodie—truthfully, if he had to pick a favorite pet, Dodie would be his choice. "I love you, my birdie. I'm just going to let you rest here for a few minutes while I look for the rats."

"Good riddance to bad rubbish," Dodie squawked.

Casey searched the apartment for thirty minutes, asking himself, *If I were a rat, where would I hide?* He apparently wasn't an expert in rat psychology because he found no trace of them. Defeated, he went back to Dodie's cage. "Dodie, I hope you didn't have anything to do with this," he said.

The bird held out his foot, his way of saying, "Take me out and play with me."

Casey couldn't resist him.

Since Casey was watching animal videos with his earbuds in, he didn't hear the shouting at first. But when he noticed Dodie acting more and more agitated, he took out the earbuds.

The voices were coming from the living room.

"I know you like to live your life like a carefree sixteen-year-old, but you can't do that when you're a parent." Casey's mom's voice.

"See, that's just like you." Casey's dad's voice. He must have come over after receiving all those texts. "You treat me like I'm a child when I'm a man. Always telling me what to do, nagging and giving orders."

"A man takes responsibility for his child," Mom said.

Casey listened. It was the same argument he had heard a hundred times. But then Casey heard his dad say something new.

"The reason I haven't sent you a check is I'm kind of between jobs right now."

Casey could hear the tension in his mom's voice. "What happened to the job at the warehouse?"

"They're totally unreasonable there. Just because one day I had been up late playing a game and I was tired—"

"You fell asleep on the job?"

"Well, just a few times."

"And so they fired you?"

"Like I said, totally unreasonable."

"Oh, no, Jason," Casey's mom said. "No no no." Casey could tell she was crying. "What are we going to do? We were barely scraping by as it was, what with what I make and the little bit of money you'd send every once in a while."

"Classic Laura," Casey's dad said, sounding disgusted. "Absolutely textbook! Always the victim—it's always about you, isn't it?"

Dodie was craning his neck and beating his wings. Casey looked at him. "You stay put. I'm going to see if I can help Mom." He couldn't let his dad talk to her like that.

Casey walked into the living room to a sight he had

seen far too many times: his dad leaning into his mom's face yelling, and his mom crying.

"Hey!" Casey said, trying to make himself heard above his dad's raised voice.

But they couldn't hear him. Casey's dad was yelling about how women trapped men and robbed them of their freedom. It was one of his more common speeches.

But then there was a sound that drowned out even Casey's dad's yelling. A high-pitched screeching accompanied by the beating of wings. Dodie flew into the living room, shrieking like an eagle, and flew directly into Casey's dad's face, his wings flapping furiously.

Casey's dad screamed—a sound Casey had never heard before.

"Dodie!" Casey yelled. "Stop! That's my dad!" No matter how angry Casey was at his dad, he couldn't let Dodie peck his eyes out or something.

Dodie kept screeching and flapping. Casey's dad's hands swatted at the bird helplessly.

Finally, Casey grabbed Dodie and pulled him off. "Shh. Shh. Settle down," he said. But Dodie was still screeching and flapping when Casey locked him into his cage and covered it.

"What the—" Casey's dad said. There was blood on the tip of his nose.

"It's my parrot," Casey said. "I think he thought you were trying to hurt Mom."

"Well, the damn thing hurt me," Casey's dad said, touching his nose, then looking at the blood on his fingers. "Hey, how did you afford a parrot anyway? I remember Casey always wanted one, and the things cost, like, a thousand dollars."

"This one was free," Casey's mom said.

"You expect me to believe that?"

"Dad, Mom wouldn't lie to you." Casey wanted to sound strong, but his voice sounded weak and pleading.

"So you say," Casey's dad said.

"Look, Jason." Mom's voice was tired. "I don't think there's anything else we can say at this point that's going to help anything. And if you don't have any money to give me right now, neither of us can make it magically appear."

In his head, Casey heard Dodie say, *You can't get blood from a turnip.*

"Maybe we should talk again after you've found another job," Casey's mom continued.

"Yeah, no pressure on me, though, right? Just make the man fix everything!" Casey's dad said, making a big show of stomping toward the door and putting on his jacket. "The next time I come back, though, you'd better keep that thing in its cage!"

After Casey's dad slammed the door, Mom started to laugh.

It was such a strange reaction that it made Casey nervous. "Mom, are you okay?"

"I'm terrible," she said, wiping her eyes. "It shouldn't be funny. It really shouldn't. But I just keep thinking of Dodie flying in here and biting your father on the nose!" She doubled over in a fit of giggles.

Casey smiled. He was too tense to laugh, but he had to admit it was kind of funny.

As Casey was getting ready for bed, the doorbell rang. His stomach knotted up. What if it was his dad again? What if he was even angrier?

Casey met his mom in the living room. She was in her pajamas and bathrobe. "If it's him again, I swear—" She looked through the peephole in the door. "Oh. It's the police."

The police? Casey couldn't decide if he should be afraid or not. He went to stand by his mom as she opened the door.

A tall, middle-aged cop stood next to a young, scrawny one.

"May I help you, officers?" Casey's mom asked.

"Ma'am," the bigger one said, "I'm Officer Watkins, and this is Officer Davis. We've had a report of a domestic disturbance. One of your neighbors said she heard yelling and some kind of high-pitched scream. We just wanted to make sure everybody was safe."

"How embarrassing," Mom said. "I was having an argument with my ex-husband, which was what the yelling was about. The high-pitched scream was my son's pet. A parrot."

"Does your ex-husband pose any physical danger to you, ma'am?" Officer Watkins asked.

"No, he's all talk."

The officer nodded like he knew the type. "Has he left the premises?"

"Yes."

"All right, well, as long as everybody's safe. Make sure you keep the noise level down, though. Too much noise and the neighbors start trying to mind your business for you."

"Yes, sir. Thank you," Mom said. After she closed the door, she turned toward Casey. "I think we should both go to bed before any new disasters befall us," she said.

In his room, Casey said good night to his frogs. He felt sad that the rats weren't there to say good night to. When he peeked inside Dodie's cage, the bird was sound asleep, probably exhausted from his earlier exertions. "Good night, Dodie," Casey whispered. "You're not allowed to bite Dad's nose again, but I know you did it because you love Mom and me."

CHAPTER 6

Dodie was a mystery. Tonight, when Casey looked into his bird's golden eyes, what he saw there felt ancient and unknowable. The more words and tricks Dodie learned and the more it seemed that he was actually participating in human conversations, the more Casey wanted to know about him. What was his history before he came to live with Casey? Did his other owners think him especially smart, even for an African grey? Had he ever shown jealousy or hostility toward any other pets or people in previous owners' households? And how old was Dodie, anyway?

"Mom?" Casey's mom was working on her laptop and squinting at whatever was on the screen. It was an old laptop, bought back in the days when money wasn't so tight.

"Mm-hm?"

"Do you still have Mr. Byron's phone number?"

"Mr. Byron?" she asked, as if she had no idea who Casey was talking about.

"You know, the old guy we got Dodie from."

"Oh, yes, of course. I'm pretty sure I still have his number in my phone. Why?"

"I was thinking of calling him. To ask him some questions about Dodie."

His mom gave him her "concerned" look. "You're not still thinking that Dodie—"

"No." He didn't want to hear his mother mention the missing rats. "It's just—he has a history. One we don't know much about. I feel like I could take better care of him if I knew more about him."

His mom smiled. "You are such a responsible pet owner, but I already knew that. I don't guess it would do any harm to call Mr. Byron and find out if he's willing to talk to you." She picked up her phone and scrolled until she said, "Aha!" and handed the phone over to him.

"Do you think it would be okay if I called him now?" Casey asked.

"Sure. It's still a reasonable hour."

Casey took the phone into the kitchen to make the

call. He couldn't explain it, but for some reason he didn't want to do it in his room. He didn't want Dodie to hear him.

"Byron residence" was how Mr. Byron answered the phone, which Casey thought was kind of weird. Old-fashioned, probably.

"Mr. Byron, this is Casey Weathers. You gave Dodie to me."

"Oh, yes, of course, Casey!" Mr. Byron said. "Is everything all right? Is Dodie behaving himself?"

Casey decided not to bring up the rats. "Yeah, Dodie's great. I've just been thinking, though . . . he has a lot of history I don't know about, and I was thinking I might want to do some research on him for a paper at school." Casey knew that adults were more likely to help you if they believed that whatever you were asking them to do related to school. "I wondered if I could maybe interview you about Dodie."

"I guess we could do that," Mr. Byron said, though he sounded a bit tentative. "There's lots I don't know, but I'm happy to share what I do know. I have to return some books to the library tomorrow. Would you like to meet there at, say, four o'clock?"

"Four o'clock sounds perfect."

Mr. Byron hadn't been kidding when he said he had to return some books to the library. He had piles of them, mystery novels and folklore collections and biographies of artists and presidents, all scattered in the back seat of his old Volvo.

"Would you like me to help you carry some of those?" Casey asked.

"That would be very helpful. Thank you, Casey."

Mr. Byron, Casey decided, looked like a shaven Santa Claus. A Santa who let his white hair grow long and stringy and didn't see anything wrong with wearing sandals with socks.

"After we drop these at the front desk, we can go into one of the private study rooms to talk," Mr. Byron said from behind his huge armload of books.

After they had found an empty study room and shut the door behind them, Casey opened his notebook and took out a pencil. If he was pretending that this was a school project, he might as well make it seem like an official interview.

"So what did you want to know about Dodie?" Mr. Byron asked.

Was it Casey's imagination, or did Mr. Byron seem nervous? "Maybe you could start out by telling me about when you first got Dodie."

"Well," Mr. Byron said, "I had Dodie for ten years.

I had been going through a really hard time right before I got him. My wife had died, and I was feeling absolutely lost. So lost that I got in the habit of taking long car drives on the weekends, often getting myself lost quite literally. One Saturday I ended up driving right across the state line and deep into Kentucky, past the Bluegrass region and into the mountains. I came across this open-air market—a flea market, I guess you'd call it—and stopped there to look around. There was an old lady—she looked like she could be a hundred—selling little things she had sewn—pot holders, dishcloths, that kind of thing. But in a cage beside her was a parrot. I stopped to look at her wares, but really what I wanted was to get a closer look at Dodie."

"So you bought Dodie from the old woman?" Casey asked.

"I didn't buy him," Mr. Byron said with a little smile. "She told me she had been looking for the right person to give this bird, and I was it. I told her she must be mistaken, that I didn't know the first thing about taking care of a bird. But she said all that could be learned. The important thing was that she knew I was suffering and this bird could help me. It was like something out of a fairy tale. I couldn't resist taking him."

Casey scribbled in his notebook. "So did Dodie help you?"

"He helped me a lot, actually. I was so lonely, and he's a lot of company, as you know. Plus, reading about parrots—their behaviors, their care—turned into an interesting project that helped distract me from my grief."

"I've read a lot about parrots since I got him, too," Casey said. "And I know parrots, especially African greys, are really smart. But did you ever feel like Dodie was extra, extra smart, even for a parrot?"

Mr. Byron nodded vigorously. "Absolutely. Sometimes we'd have these—well, they were conversations, really—that were so sophisticated I couldn't believe I was chatting with a bird. There would be real back-and-forth, you know, just like a human conversation. And he knows all these old Appalachian ballads—'Pretty Polly,' 'In the Pines,' 'Knoxville Girl'—that I guess he learned from Mrs. Smalls, the woman who gave him to me. But there's more to it than just intelligence, though, don't you think? I mean, Dodie is emotionally complex."

"What do you mean?" Casey asked.

"Hmm . . ." Mr. Byron stroked his beard. "I guess I mean that if Dodie loves you, then he really loves you. But if he hates you . . ." He trailed off, looking like he was lost in a memory. "And he'd hold on to feelings for a long time. Like if he got mad about something, he'd stay angry for days. As if he were a person. A bad-tempered person sometimes. Other animals I've been around get mad sometimes, but they don't hold grudges."

"Right." Casey thought about Dodie's resentment of the rats. He wondered what his mom would think if she heard Mr. Byron's description of Dodie. Would she think he was anthropomorphizing? "Mr. Byron, do you have contact information for Mrs. Smalls? I'd like to interview her, too. Maybe I could email her."

Mr. Byron chuckled. "I would be shocked if Mrs. Smalls had a computer. I think I might still have her address if you're comfortable with something as old-fashioned as writing her a letter. Though, to be honest, I don't know if she's even still alive."

"Mr. Byron"—Casey gathered his courage to ask the question he had been saving for last—"did you really get rid of Dodie because you were having health problems and couldn't take care of him?"

Mr. Byron shifted in his seat and couldn't seem to quite meet Casey's eyes. "Well, certainly, that was part of it. A big part. I had been ill and had a brief hospital stay and was adjusting to some new medication. All those were contributing factors."

"But that's not the whole story, is it?" Casey said.

"No," Mr. Byron said. "But please know I wouldn't

have given you Dodie if I thought I was putting you in any danger. It was just that there were some incidents with Dodie that were . . . unsettling. One in particular."

"Please tell me."

"I won't take him back, you know," Mr. Byron said.

"I wouldn't ask you to take him back," Casey said. "I love Dodie." It was true, but there was still a knot of anxiety in his stomach about whatever Mr. Byron was about to tell him.

"It was my cat, Thomas Aquinas," Mr. Byron said with a tremor in his voice. "A friendly orange fellow. Dodie hated him. I know that in nature cats and birds aren't the best of friends, but I had hoped they could at least peacefully coexist. My hopes were in vain. Dodie blinded him."

"He what?" Casey felt like his heart had jumped in his mouth.

"One day he was mocking the cat, saying, 'Stop looking at me.' Thomas hissed at Dodie, and Dodie flew at him all of a sudden, and scratched his eyes. It was horrible. I got Thomas to the vet right away, but they couldn't save his sight." Mr. Byron swallowed hard. "He does remarkably well, though. Cats have such heightened senses that they can still function quite normally when one sense is taken away. He can still find his way around, even jump up onto places I don't want him to. If his eyes weren't stitched shut to protect the sockets, you'd never know he was blind."

Casey felt sick with horror. He couldn't make himself speak, so he just nodded.

"I scolded Dodie about it, of course," Mr. Byron said. "I said he should be ashamed of what he had done to the poor kitty. But Dodie just said, 'He kept looking at me.'"

CHAPTER 7

W ho is Minnie Smalls?" Casey's mom asked when she came back in from checking the mail.

Casey looked up from the penguin documentary he was watching on the Animal Channel. It took him a second to remember the answer to the question. He had written Mrs. Smalls over a week ago without really expecting a response, without knowing if she was even still alive. "Oh, she was the lady who owned Dodie before Mr. Byron. I wrote her a letter."

"Well, it looks like she wrote you back," Mom said, handing him an envelope. "You're really doing some detective work on Dodie, aren't you?"

"It's interesting," Casey said. He took the letter to his room and sat down on the bed. He didn't know why, but he felt the need to be alone when he read it. Casey typically didn't receive much mail. Usually it was just once a year when he got birthday cards with birthday money from his grandparents. The writing on the envelope was shaky, clearly the work of an elderly person. He opened the envelope and pulled out a sheet of lined notebook paper, the same kind he used for school, and unfolded it to read the spidery handwriting.

Dear Casey,

I received your letter with surprise. Polly was the parrot's name when I had him, but I gave him away more than ten years ago. I haven't forgotten him, though. I loved that bird. It sounds like you're taking good care of him, which I am glad to hear.

Even though it has been a long time since I had Polly I will try to answer your questions. He was the only bird I ever had, so I didn't know if he was smarter than other birds. I knew he was real smart, though. I have always liked to sing when doing chores around the house. I sing the old songs my mama taught me that her mama had taught her before. Dodie learned all those songs real fast, so most of what you hear him sing he probably learned off me. He talked a lot, too. He repeated things I taught him like "hello" and "pretty bird," but sometimes it felt like he could talk back and forth with you like a regular person. I didn't think this was normal for a bird, but I lived alone except for Polly back then and he was good company.

You asked me where I got Polly and if I know how old he is. I got Polly in 1975. I was a young woman then. My husband and I had just moved from Kentucky to Ohio because he got a job in a factory up there. I had never lived in an apartment or in a city before, and I was lonesome and homesick. I've always liked to sew, and there was a little sewing shop in walking distance of the apartment. I went there just about every day. Just looking at familiar things like fabric and spools of thread made me feel less lost somehow.

The shop was called Just Sew-Sew, which I thought was cute. It was run by a Polish woman named Maria Wachowski. I know it makes me sound like a hillbilly, but she was the first person from a foreign country I ever met. She was kind and easy to talk to. One day when I went in there, I was feeling particularly sad and I told her how lonesome I was especially with my husband gone all day. She said, "I know what you need." She went in the back of the store where she lived with her family in a little apartment. When she came back, she was carrying a big cage with a gray parrot with a red tail inside it.

I thought he was the prettiest thing I'd ever seen. She told me, "I can't take care of him anymore. He will be a good friend to you."

Polly was a good friend and he made me a lot less lonesome. I only ended up living in the city for a year, though, because my husband got killed in a car wreck. I went back home to Kentucky with Polly and a new baby. I moved into a little house on my family's property and took care of my little boy, getting by taking in sewing for people. I took care of Polly, but in a lot of ways he took care of me, too. He was a good guard for the property on account of being so loud, and some days he was the closest thing I had to another adult to talk to. Me and Polly would sing to little Robbie while I worked on my sewing. We lived that way for many years.

You also asked why I got rid of Polly. I've never told anybody this and am afraid you'll think me foolish or crazy. Polly took a dislike to my son, Robbie. He was a sweet baby but starting when he was a teenager he got harder and harder to get along with, and when he and I would get into an argument, Polly would get real mad, beating his wings and screaming. When Robbie was in his thirties, he worked in the mines, and it got so every time Robbie would come over Polly would start singing this song about a mining disaster. I don't know where he learned it because I didn't teach it to him, but the song was about an explosion in the mines where a bunch of miners get killed. He'd sing it over and over when Robbie was around and Robbie would get mad and tell me to shut that bird up.

But then there was explosion in the mine where Robbie worked. It happened just like in the song Polly would sing. Robbie wasn't one of the miners who got killed, but he did lose a leg and wasn't able to work anymore. He believed Polly caused the disaster. When I asked him how a bird could've done that, he'd say, "I don't know how he did it, but he did it." Every time Robbie came over, Polly would yell, "Peg leg! Peg leg!" at him. I don't know where he learned that either, but it was awful. Robbie said that the bird was possessed by the devil and that he was going to wring its neck. I felt like I had to give away Polly to keep him safe. But somehow I felt like giving him away was keeping Robbie safe, too, even though that doesn't make any sense.

I hope that answers all your questions. And I hope you're asking them just because you're curious and not because anything bad has happened. You seem like a nice boy. I will pray for you.

Sincerely,
Mrs. Minnie Smalls

Casey read the letter straight through, then read it three more times. It was too much to take in. How she got Dodie. The weirdness of Dodie singing about an explosion in a mine and then an explosion actually happening. And how old was Dodie anyway? Mrs. Smalls got him in 1975, and he wasn't a baby because he had been Mrs. Wachowski's pet before. At the very youngest, Dodie was in his mid- to late forties.

On a whim, Casey opened his laptop and typed "Just Sew-Sew" and "Cincinnati" into a search engine. Shockingly, a store with that name still existed. Theresa Wachowski was listed as the owner. The daughter of the woman who gave Dodie to Mrs. Smalls? Casey wondered. He wrote a message to the store's email address:

Dear Ms. Wachowski,

I know this is kind of weird and out of nowhere but I am the owner of an African grey parrot that I think might have belonged to someone in your family years ago. I am curious if this is the same parrot and if you might have any memories of him.

Thank you,
Casey Weathers

"Breakfast for dinner's ready!" Mom called, sounding extra cheerful.

Mom always acted like breakfast for dinner was a big fun event, but Casey knew it was what she did toward the end of the month when there wasn't any money for groceries. He liked pancakes, though, so he wasn't complaining.

After plowing through a stack of pancakes, he went back to his room to take care of the pets, but first he checked his email just in case Ms. Wachowski had written him back.

She had. It was a two-sentence message: *My mother got that bird in 1940, a few years after she immigrated to America. How can that thing still be alive?*

Feeling shaky, Casey typed *life-span of African grey parrot in captivity* into the search engine. The answer *40–60 years* popped up. If what Theresa Wachowski said was true, then Dodie was way, way past his expiration date.

Casey walked over to Dodie's cage. Dodie stuck out his foot.

"You want to get out and play?" Casey said. It was a question he asked Dodie on a daily basis, but tonight when he asked it, his voice shook.

"Play with my boy!" Dodie said. For a second, Casey just stared at the bird. His feathers were sleek and supple; his eyes were bright. He looked young and healthy. He didn't look like a bird that had lived many decades past his species' life-span.

Casey opened the cage and let Dodie perch on his forearm. Soon Dodie had climbed up to Casey's shoulder and was nuzzling his hair and murmuring, "My boy, my boy." Casey wondered if Dodie had done the same thing to Mr. Byron, to Mrs. Smalls, to Maria Wachowski.

"How old are you, Dodie?" Casey whispered. "How long have you been here?"

"I've always been," Dodie crooned back at him. "Always."

Casey felt a shiver run through him. "So you've just gone from person to person for, like, hundreds of years?"

"I go where I'm needed," Dodie said, nuzzling Casey's neck.

Casey didn't know how to feel. Scared, yes, but also fascinated to have such a remarkable pet. More than remarkable. Magical. And really, what did he have to be scared of? Didn't Dodie love him? "Dodie, Mom and I are safe, right? I mean, you love us, don't you?"

"Yes," Dodie whispered in his ear. "Love you. Always."

CHAPTER 8

"T his can't be good," Casey's mom said. There was
an edge of tension in her voice.

Casey felt a prickle of anxiety. "What's that?"

"Your dad just texted and said he's coming over."
Mom frowned down at her phone.

"I don't guess it's so he can take me to the zoo,"
Casey said. Dodie was standing on the couch next
to Casey, playing with a baby's shape sorter toy Casey
had found for him at a thrift store. Dodie picked up a
triangular block with his beak and dropped it into
the triangular hole. Next, he dropped a square block
in a square hole. He would play with the thing for
hours, obsessively sorting by shape and color.

"Yeah, I wouldn't hold my breath." She glanced at

Dodie and sighed. "I hate to interrupt Dodie's fun, but maybe you'd better put him in his cage. If you recall, the last time things didn't go so well between him and your dad."

"True," Casey said. He held out his arm. "Come on, Dodie." Dodie perched on Casey's arm, and Casey carried him into his room. He put some pumpkin seeds in Dodie's dish to keep him busy, then put Dodie in his cage and locked it. "I'll get you back out as soon as he's gone, my birdie."

Soon there was a knock at the door. Casey came back out into the living room.

"Why don't you answer it? At least he likes you," Mom said. "If he sees me first thing, he'll just get mad."

Casey wasn't really sure how much his dad liked him, but he still went to the door.

"Hey, dude," his dad said, holding up his hand for a high five. He looked a little more disheveled than usual. He clearly hadn't shaved for a few days, and his floppy hair was lank and in need of a shampoo.

Casey gave him his usual half-hearted high five. "Hi, Dad."

"I need to talk to your mom for a few minutes, buddy."

"Sure." Casey headed toward his room.

"But maybe you should stay," Casey's dad said, "since it concerns you, too."

"Okay." Casey glanced over at his mom. She was biting her lower lip like she did when she was nervous.

They all sat down in the living room. It felt oddly formal, like they were people who didn't know each other that well and were about to have tea and crumpets or something.

"So basically," Casey's dad said, propping his feet up on the coffee table, "I just swung by to let you know I'm moving."

Casey wasn't sure what he meant by moving. "You mean, to a different apartment?" Actually, it would be nice if his dad moved into a better apartment. The one he lived in was in the basement of an old house, and it always smelled like mildew and old socks.

"To a different state, dude," he said like it was no big deal. "The job thing wasn't happening here, but I got a lead on a sweet construction gig out in Texas. It pays in cash."

"Oh, I get it," Casey's mom said. "If you get paid under the table, you think you can get out of paying child support."

"Well, I've been thinking about that," Casey's dad said. "And I think it's time that we all work on being more independent. Laura, you have your job and you'll get an even better one once you graduate from college. I'll have my job in Texas, and then in a couple of years, Casey will be old enough to get a job himself—"

"Jason." Casey's mom's voice was icy. "Even if Casey does decide to get an after-school job when he's older, it won't pay enough to cover his food and clothes and medical care. You owe me a monthly child support payment. It's the law."

Casey's dad smiled the smile that he used when he wanted to be charming. Casey had seen him pull out this trick many times, whether it was with Casey's mom or a bill collector. "Didn't Martin Luther King, Jr. say that 'an unjust law is no law at all'?"

Casey's mom sprang to her feet. Her eyes flashed with anger in a way that reminded Casey of Dodie. "What kind of a jerk uses a quote from one of the greatest human rights leaders of all time as a way to justify not paying child support? Really, Jason, just when I think you've hit the bottom, you somehow manage to fall even farther."

"If I'm falling," Casey's dad said, "it's because you pushed me."

Casey was experiencing what had been a frequent occurrence when his mom and dad had still lived together. He would look at one and then the other as they volleyed accusations and insults back and forth. It was like being a spectator at the world's most miserable tennis match.

"Look," Casey's dad said, rising to his feet. "People make mistakes. And when I married you, I made a big one. Does that mean I should have to pay for that mistake for the rest of my life?"

"It's not about me. It's about Casey and making sure he has what he needs. Regardless of how things were with you and me, Casey is not a mistake," Mom said. Her words dripped icicles.

Casey's dad held up his hands as if in surrender. "Hey, don't take this the wrong way, Casey, but when I look at you, I don't see any of myself, you know? Maybe there isn't any of me in you."

If Casey's mom had been icy before, now she was white-hot with anger. "Jason, what are you implying?"

"I'm not implying anything, but what I'm saying is that it's time for me to start a new chapter. I need to turn the page." His voice was getting louder and louder. Casey could hear Dodie from behind the closed door of his room, screeching and beating his wings. "You know what? I may not take that job in Texas. I might work in a salmon fishery in Alaska. I might go down to Mexico. Who knows? Wherever I end up, I'm not telling you about it!" He stomped to the door.

Casey's mom followed him. "Jason, can't we sit down calmly and talk about this like adults? Can't you be an adult for once?" Her voice broke, the way it did when she was trying not to cry.

"I am being an adult, Laura," Casey's dad said. "I am independent. I make my own choices. I am declaring myself a free man!" He slammed the door in his ex-wife's face.

Casey wanted to be strong for his mom, but it was hard not to cry. For all of his faults, Casey's dad was still his dad. If he was going to leave forever, it seemed like the least he could do was look Casey in the face and say goodbye.

"Unreal," Casey's mom said, sinking into the chair. "I'm sorry you had to be there for that ugly scene."

"It's okay," Casey said, even though it wasn't.

"I guess I can get a lawyer," Casey's mom said. "But I don't know how I'd pay one. What is it Dodie says? 'You can't get blood from a turnip'?"

"Oh, Dodie!" Casey said, remembering that the bird was still locked in his cage. "I guess I can get him back out now." To tell the truth, he was happy for an excuse to leave the room where the big blowup had occurred, even if it was just for a couple of minutes.

"Yeah, the coast is clear now," Casey's mom said. "Though, to be honest, I would've loved it if Dodie had come flying out of your room and given your dad one last good chomp on the nose!"

When Casey walked up to Dodie's cage, the first thing he noticed was that the door was open. The second thing he noticed was that Dodie was not inside.

But it was the third thing that was the most disturbing. The window in his room was wide open, even though Casey was sure he hadn't opened the window— and that he'd locked Dodie's cage like always. The breeze blew the white curtains, making them look like ghosts. Casey searched the room frantically, but he knew it was useless.

Dodie was gone.

CHAPTER 9

I don't know what the right thing to do is," Casey said. "Should I leave the window open?" They had looked all over the apartment for Dodie and hadn't seen or heard him, but it wasn't impossible that he could still be hiding somewhere, right? If Dodie was inside and Casey left the window open, the bird could get out. But if the bird was outside and Casey closed the window, then he couldn't get in.

"Leave it open," his mom said. "I think the chances are better that he's outside than that he's in. If the window's open, he can fly back in when he gets tired or hungry."

Casey and his mom and Ari had spent two hours walking around the apartment complex and the neighborhood looking for Dodie. They had called his name and tried to lure him with fresh fruit and sunflower seeds, but they hadn't seen any sign of him. As Casey's mom had said, if you didn't have wings yourself, it was awfully hard to find an animal that could fly.

"I hope so," Casey said. "But after tonight, I feel like I'm all out of hope." How could your father and your pet abandon you on the same night?

"It's been a terrible night," Casey's mom admitted. "Maybe if we go to bed, things will look better in the morning."

Casey didn't feel comforted. He figured that was just the kind of thing you had to say if you were a mom.

He went to bed, but he didn't sleep. He was too hurt by his father and too worried about Dodie. He lay on his back and stared at the ceiling. It felt like his eyes were physically incapable of closing.

The doorbell rang and Casey jumped like a bomb had exploded. He looked at his alarm clock. It was 12:47. He got out of bed in time to meet his mother at the front door. She looked through the peephole. "Great," she said. "The police again."

It was the same officers who had come to the door before, the tall one and the skinny one.

"Let me guess," Casey's mom said. "Noise complaint again?"

"No, ma'am," Officer Watkin said. "May we come in?"

"Of course." Casey could hear the fear in his mom's voice as she stepped aside to let the officers in and then closed the door behind them.

"Are you the wife of Jason Weathers?" Officer Davis asked.

"The ex-wife," Casey's mom said.

Officer Watkins took off his hat. "I'm sorry to have to tell you this, ma'am, but there was an accident. Mr. Weathers seemed to have lost control of his vehicle. It was strange. No other cars were involved. His vehicle ran off the road at a stretch where no guardrails were present. The car probably flipped over at least twice as it fell down the side of the hill. Mr. Weathers wasn't wearing a seat belt. He was pronounced dead at the scene. We found your contact information on his phone."

"I . . . I don't know what to say," Casey's mom said. "We had argued earlier, and he left here angry, but that still doesn't explain—"

"I know," the officer said. "Accidents are mysterious sometimes." He looked down at Casey. "Are you—"

"His son," Casey said. He felt strangely numb, like things were unfolding in one of those dreams in which you were more of an observer than a participant.

"I'm sorry," Officer Watkins said. "I know this is hard. I lost my dad when I was about your age." He looked back at Casey's mom. "I know this may be painful, but in the morning, could you come to the morgue to identify the body?"

Casey's mom nodded. "Yes. Of course."

After the officers left, Casey and his mom sat at the kitchen table in stunned silence. Finally, she said, "Would you like a cup of chamomile tea?"

"Sure, thanks," Casey said. He didn't especially want tea, but he felt like they both needed something to do. If his mom made tea and he drank it, at least they'd both be doing something.

Once his mom set two steaming mugs on the table, she said, "You know, I spent a lot of time thinking angry, unkind thoughts about your father, but I never wished him dead."

"I know that, Mom."

She reached out and put her hand on his. "How are you feeling right now?"

"I don't know, to be honest," Casey said. "I think I'm still in shock."

His mom nodded. "Me too."

The truth, though Casey couldn't bring himself to say it, was that in some ways things didn't feel that different than before. His dad had never been there for either of them, really. In one way or another, he had always been gone.

Now Casey and his mom would take care of each other, just like they always had.

"You know, I feel terrible for even bringing this up," his mom said. "But unless he wrote us out of it, there is a life insurance policy. And knowing how your dad never got around to doing things, I bet he never changed the policy. It's for quite a bit of money. Enough to make things easier. It's too bad he had to die to help us out financially."

Casey nodded. Was it terrible that in some ways he felt sadder about losing Dodie than he did about losing his dad? He was sure that it was. But at the same time, his feelings kind of made sense. He had known that Dodie had loved him. He couldn't say the same about his dad.

"You look tired," Mom said.

"I am. Don't know if I'll be able to sleep, though."

"Why don't you go lie down and see what happens? If you can't sleep, come find me. I'll probably be up for the rest of the night, but I'd feel better if you could get some rest."

"Okay, Mom." He kissed her cheek. "I love you." He didn't say it often enough.

"I love you more."

Casey lay in bed, wishing he could lose consciousness but knowing he wouldn't be able to. He should stay in bed, though, just to let his mom think he had managed to get some sleep.

A whooshing sound made him turn his head toward the window. A shadowy shape landed on the window-sill, then flew straight to the birdcage.

"Dodie?" Casey turned on his bedside lamp.

The bird was sitting on his perch in his cage, swing-ing on his perch and singing, *"Then he stabbed her in the heart till her heart's blood did flow / And into the grave Pretty Polly did go."*

Casey jumped up and slammed the window shut, then he ran to the cage. "Dodie, are you all right?"

Dodie kept on singing. "Now, a debt to the Devil, that Willy must pay / For killing Pretty Polly and running away."

The bird's tail was always scarlet, but now some-thing had stained his talons and wings red, too. It was a rusty red, wet and sticky.

Casey was afraid that he understood. *Was that blood?* "Dodie, what happened to my dad? Did you have something to do with it?"

"Good riddance to bad rubbish," Dodie squawked.

He held out his foot, indicating that he'd like to sit on Casey's arm.

Casey didn't know how to feel. He imagined Dodie flying into his dad's car window, flapping his wings, blocking his dad's vision, biting and scratching. It wasn't right, but had Dodie done it because, between his human-like brain and animal morality, he had believed he was helping Casey?

When Casey looked into Dodie's intelligent golden eyes, he didn't see anything cold or calculating—he saw more love and devotion than he had ever seen from his father.

Casey's arm shook, but he held it out. Dodie stepped onto Casey's forearm, then climbed up to his shoulder, leaving four-toed red footprints up the sleeve of Casey's pajamas. Soon Dodie was nuzzling Casey's hair, a sensation that felt comforting and familiar.

"My birdie," Casey heard himself whispering.

"My boy," Dodie crooned in Casey's ear. "*My* boy."

KEEP READING

FOR A PREVIEW OF THE SECOND

CREEPSHOW™ COLLECTION

THE CURSED

CHAPTER 1

"Pardon me, ma'am," Randy said as he reached under the hen and retrieved a fresh-laid egg. He gently placed the egg in his basket and gave the butterscotch-colored bird a little pat. "Good girl, Anne Francis."

Randy had named all the hens after the stars of the movies he saw on the Saturdays when he got to go to town. Anne Francis played Altaira in *Forbidden Planet*, and Randy thought she was one of the most beautiful women he had ever seen. He called the arrogant black rooster, who sometimes charged up on him and pecked his legs, Godzilla. He knew that the rooster would stomp around and destroy cities, too, if he wasn't just a regular-sized chicken. Two of the other hens, Zsa Zsa and Eva, were named after the glamorous Gabor sisters who were always on the covers of the gossip magazines.

"Zsa Zsa's a good girl," Randy said, stroking the hen's soft white feathers. Daddy said it was foolish to name the chickens, that they were livestock, not pets. But Momma said she didn't see any harm in it, that Randy was still a child and children were supposed to have lively imaginations.

Daddy always said the same thing in response: "Randy is thirteen years old. I was already working in the mines when I was his age."

But Daddy didn't work in the mines anymore. Neither did any of the other men in the county. The mines had shut down two years ago, in 1954, and as a result, families that used to have enough food on the table and some extra money for Saturday movies and ice cream now had very little. It was the same all over the coal country of West Virginia, and boys like Randy who always figured they'd be miners once they left school now didn't know what they were going to be.

Randy moved on to Eva and wondered if she'd always known it would be her life's purpose to lay eggs, and if she liked her job. She was certainly good at it; she had an egg for Randy every single evening.

The truth was that while Randy missed the more frequent trips to the movie house and the soda fountain since Daddy lost his job, he wasn't sad that his future wasn't all planned out for him anymore. He had never wanted to be a miner, never wanted to make his living doing back-breaking labor in a dark, dangerous hole in the ground. He didn't want to live with the constant cough his daddy had from the dark and the damp, didn't want his fingernails to be permanently stained black no matter how much he scrubbed them.

"What do you think I ought to do with myself?" Randy asked Eva. It was a rhetorical question but one that Randy thought about a lot. He liked taking care of the farm animals, but based on how his parents were struggling, he didn't see a future in farming. Daddy had to take on odd jobs just to make ends meet.

That being said, Randy didn't know what he wanted to be. He was old enough to know he couldn't be a space explorer or a cowboy or a jungle adventurer, but still, there had to be something better than what he was doing now, helping his family barely eke out an existence on their little plot of land in a remote hollow surrounded by mountains.

Randy finished gathering the eggs from the other chickens named after movie stars, then scattered cracked corn on the ground. "There you go, ladies and gentleman," he said. The chickens pecked at the corn, making satisfied little chortling noises.

Randy made his way past the barn, where Maybelle the cow (Randy's momma had named her) was chewing her cud, and up to their little unpainted wooden house. Rufus, their black-and-tan hound, was on the porch, gnawing on a bone from the ham hock that had gone into tonight's pot of soup beans.

"How many eggs?" Momma said when Randy came into the house. She was washing the supper dishes at the sink. Her chestnut brown hair was coming loose from the bun she always wore it in. Momma was a pretty woman, but ever since the mines closed, she looked tired.

"Eighteen," he said, setting the basket down on the kitchen table.

"Not bad," she said. "Some to eat and some to sell."

"Yes'm," Randy said, putting the clean dishes she had just dried into the cabinet.

"You got lessons tonight?" Momma asked. She always called homework *lessons*. She and Daddy both talked more country and old-fashioned than Randy did.

"I've got a little homework," Randy said.

Momma nodded. "Best get to it, then. I'll finish up here."

Because their house had only two small bedrooms, Randy shared his room with his five-year-old sister, Cindy. Mama had sewn a privacy curtain and hung it in the middle of the room so it was "just like you each have a room of your own." It wasn't really. But Cindy had an earlier bedtime than Randy and was a sound sleeper, so he could sit on his side of the room and do his homework or even listen to his transistor radio softly while she snoozed away.

Randy tried to pay attention to his math homework, but numbers never held his interest. He liked stories and excitement. Sometimes there were what the teacher called "story problems" in math, but the stories were boring, about how much of something somebody had or how fast a train was going. Instead of thinking about the train in the math problem, Randy fantasized about jumping on a high-speed locomotive and riding it all the way to Huntington or maybe even Cincinnati.

His fantasy was interrupted by a soft rapping on his window. "Shh," he hissed, afraid that the noise would wake Cindy.

He looked through the window. Bill, his best friend, who lived in the house across the road, pressed his face against the glass. Bill stretched out his mouth with his fingers and stuck out his tongue. "I'm the boogeyman come to get you!" he said, laughing.

Randy rolled his eyes and pushed up the window. "You're the sorriest excuse for a boogeyman I ever did see," he said. "Now don't make too much racket. Cindy's asleep."

Bill climbed in through the window and took a seat on Randy's bed. Like Randy, Bill was clean but poor looking. He had patches on the knees of his britches, and his sneakers were falling apart at the seams. But just about everybody Randy and Bill knew looked like this. Being poor wasn't as big a deal when everybody else was poor, too.

"You could use the door to come in, you know," Randy said, sitting down next to Bill.

"Yeah, but if I did your momma would know I was here, and she might tell my momma that I'm here. And strictly speaking, I ain't supposed to be here." He grinned, showing the gap between his two front teeth.

"And where are you supposed to be at?" Randy asked.

"Home in bed without supper," Bill said. "On account of that stunt I pulled in school. Say, you ain't got any leftover corn bread, do you?"

"We might. Sit tight. I'll be right back." Randy went into the kitchen. A few slices' worth of corn bread were in the cast-iron skillet sitting on the back of the stove. He cut off a hunk and got a glass of milk from the refrigerator, the appliance which Momma and Daddy still called "the icebox." Momma and Daddy were sitting on the couch listening to the radio. Daddy's job loss had killed any chance Randy's family had of owning a television any time soon.

"Growing boy, huh?" Momma said, nodding toward the snack Randy was holding.

"Yes, ma'am," he said, hightailing it to his room. He hadn't lied, exactly. He just hadn't said who the growing boy in question was.

"Thanks, buddy," Bill said, snatching the corn bread and the glass. "It don't hardly seem right, starving a feller half to death just cause he's a little high-spirited."

Randy smiled. "And leaving a cow pie in the seat of the teacher's desk—that was being high-spirited?"

Bill grinned. "It was."

"And so was beating up Carl Pruitt for telling on you?"

Bill nodded, his mouth full of corn bread. After he swallowed, he said, "That kid had it coming. There's something I don't trust about him. Between you and me, I think he's a communist."

Randy held back the urge to roll his eyes. This was not an unusual statement from Bill. He thought everybody he disliked was a communist. "Carl Pruitt? Really?" Randy said.

Bill nodded again. "They're everywhere, you know."

Randy had heard a lot in school about Russia and how bad communism was and how there were Americans who were members of the communist party trying to infiltrate normal American towns. Still, Randy wasn't as convinced as Bill that the regular people they met were communists in disguise. Why would anybody want to infiltrate a place as small and insignificant as Green Mountain, West Virginia?

"So I was thinking we might go camping on Saturday night," Bill said.

This was one of the reasons Bill was Randy's best friend even if they didn't always agree on everything. Bill could always think of fun things for them to do. "Camping, huh?" Randy said.

"Sure, my brother said we could use his pup tent. We've got a roll of baloney and some crackers at our house, so I could bring some of them. And maybe you could get your momma to boil some eggs and fix us a jug of fresh milk. We could stay up late as we want and tell ghost stories, and in the morning maybe we could walk over to Hatcher's Pond and go fishing."

It might not be an adventure like he'd see on the movie screen, but it was better than staying home and feeding the chickens. "Let's do it," Randy said. "If my folks say it's all right."

"They will," Bill said. "Your folks is way less mean than mine. Speaking of that, I'd better get home and in bed before I get caught, or they won't let me out to do nothing."

Bill was halfway out the window when Cindy, from the other side of the room, called, "Good night, Bill."

"Good night, Cindy," Bill said. "Sorry I woke you up sneaking in like I did."

"It's okay," Cindy said. "I won't tell on you. I ain't no communist."

CHAPTER 2

Daddy was sitting in the living room reading the newspaper. "Y'all gonna do any hunting while you're up there? Lots of rabbit this time of year."

Randy was rolling up a blanket and a pillow. It was the best he could do since he didn't have a sleeping bag. "No, sir, but we might do some fishing in the morning."

Daddy nodded and turned his attention back to the paper. "Try to catch us something good, then."

Momma came into the living room carrying a paper grocery bag. "All right, I fixed you three boiled eggs apiece and a jug of milk to share. There's also four cold biscuits with jelly."

"Thank you, Momma." The biscuits and jelly were

an unexpected bonus. It would be nice to have something sweet.

Momma's brow wrinkled a little. "Now you boys be careful in them woods. There's all kinds of wild animals there, and I worry about you'uns being up there by yourselves—"

Daddy looked up from his paper. "He's thirteen years old, Alma."

Momma smiled and shook her head. "I know, I know. And you was working in the mines when you was thirteen."

There was a pounding on the door that could only be Bill.

Randy ran to open it and found his friend, loaded down with camping gear. "Hey. You ready?" he asked. Randy could tell Bill was buzzing with excitement.

"Be careful, and have fun," Momma said.

The boys headed off in the direction of the woods while Bill recited the food items he was carrying. "I've got a half a pound of baloney, a full sleeve of saltine crackers, a can of pork 'n' beans, and four big dill pickles."

Randy listed the contents of the sack Momma had packed for them.

"Shoot," Bill said, grinning. "We're gonna have us a big old picnic, ain't we?"

"Yep." It was a beautiful day, the temperature warm

but not hot, the sunlight bright but not blinding. Randy felt good walking into the woods with his best friend, walking toward adventure and away from chores and schoolwork. They hadn't even set up camp yet, and he was already having fun.

Once they were in the woods, they had to watch their step. It was an uphill walk, and the ground was treacherous with rocks and roots and twisting vines. It was pretty, though. Randy liked the way the sunlight shone through the trees, liked the sounds of the birds and the squirrels chirping and chittering. He liked how in some places, the moss formed a soft green carpet under his feet.

"Snake," Bill whispered.

"Where at?" Randy whispered back.

"Over yonder," Bill said, pointing.

On a big flat rock, a long black snake was stretched out, letting a sunbeam shine on him.

"Aw, that's just a black snake," Randy said. "He don't mean no harm unless you're a mouse or a rat. He's just getting a suntan, that's all."

Bill laughed. "How can a snake get a suntan?"

After a few more minutes of walking, they came to a clearing where the ground was surprisingly level. "You reckon this is our spot?" Bill asked.

"Looks like it to me," Randy said.

They set up the pup tent together, then gathered wood to start a campfire. Once the fire was going, Bill took out the pork 'n' beans, a can opener, and a small pan. They cooked the beans over the open fire, taking turns holding the pan just above the flame, until they got bored with the process and ate the beans cold out of the pan. Bill had neglected to bring spoons, so they tilted the pan up to their mouths and slurped. After that, they ate some baloney and crackers and a boiled egg and two dill pickles each, then passed the milk jug back and forth.

Randy patted his belly. "I'm full as a tick."

"Me too," Bill said. "Why don't we save the biscuits and jelly for after it gets dark, when we're telling ghost stories?"

"Good idea," Randy said. It felt good to be full. Since his daddy had lost his job, there had been nights when he'd gone to bed still hungry. Not because there'd been no food—Momma always managed to put something on the table—but because there hadn't been enough to sate his appetite. Like Momma said, he was a growing boy.

When darkness came upon them, it was so complete it was like a giant pair of hands had dropped a big black blanket over them. If it weren't for the flashlight Randy had packed and the campfire they had built, they wouldn't have been able to see their hands in front of them.

"Now it's time for spooky stories," Bill said.

Randy told a story his granny used to tell him about a ghost who haunted an old woman and kept telling her "I want my big toe!" It was a ghost story, but it was more funny than scary. Bill told a story about Old Raw Hide and Bloody Bones, who killed and ate children.

"My daddy always told me about Old Raw Hide and Bloody Bones," Randy said. "He said he came to get little boys that wouldn't go to bed when they was supposed to."

"Mine told me the same thing!" Bill said, laughing. "That's why grown-ups make up them stories—to scare you into doing what they want you to do. I never believed 'em, though."

"I did, when I was little," Randy said. "I figure just about every other kid in West Virginia believed Old Raw Hide and Bloody Bones was hiding under their bed at one time or another."

"Not me, though," Bill said.

"Not ever?" Surely, Randy thought, there was one time during Bill's childhood when he had been afraid of a strangely moving shadow that turned out to be a tree branch outside. There had to have been a time or two when he lay curled in a ball in bed because of the fear that something hiding underneath might grab his ankle.

"Nope," Bill said. "I ain't no chicken. I don't want to be like that weird kid in school, James, who's always going on about monsters and ghosts, saying they're real."

"He is kind of . . . different," Randy said. James had moved to Green Mountain from Cincinnati at the beginning of the school year. Maybe it was because he was a city kid who talked and dressed different from everybody else, but he was definitely having a hard time making friends. He always sat at lunch by himself reading *Famous Monsters of Filmland* magazine. Randy felt sorry for him. He seemed lonely.

"He's a chicken is what he is," Bill said. "Always scaring himself about things that ain't real. I figure a chicken's about the worst thing you can be, besides a communist."

"Hey, I like chickens," Randy said. "I spend time with them every day."

"That don't mean you want to be one," Bill said.

"No, that's true." Randy had to admit that calling somebody a chicken because they were cowardly made a lot of sense. Chickens were scared of everything— noises, falling leaves, their own reflections. But they had a right to be scared. Nearly every other living creature wanted to eat them.

"Hey, you reckon it's time to eat those biscuits and jelly?" Bill asked.

"Sure."

The boys ate their biscuits, watching the last embers of the campfire die down and wiping their hands on their trousers mostly because their mommas weren't there to tell them not to. Then they doused the fire with a pan of water from the nearby creek, kicked dirt over it, and stomped it down to make sure no embers were burning. Then, with only the beam from Randy's flashlight to guide them, they crawled into the pup tent and snuggled down into their nest of blankets. Randy could feel every root and rock on the ground beneath his back, but somehow the tent was still cozy, maybe because Bill was right there with him.

Randy had almost settled into sleep when he heard a rustling outside. Something brushed against the outside of the tent. "Did you hear that?"

"Yeah." Bill's voice was fuzzy with sleep. "It's probably just a possum. Or if we're unlucky, a skunk."

Randy hoped it wasn't a skunk. Rufus the hound dog had gotten sprayed by a skunk once, and Randy had had to give him a bath with tomato juice. It had helped a little, but he still stank.

Whatever was outside the tent pushed it harder, almost collapsing one side.

"Uh . . . that's something bigger than a possum," Randy said. His heart beat faster. There were coyotes in the woods and sometimes bears.

"You reckon we should crawl out of the tent?" Bill asked. His voice sounded like he was wide awake now.

"We'd better. That way we can run if we have to." They were sitting ducks in the pup tent. Well, lying-down ducks, which was even worse.

Randy crawled out of the tent, holding the flashlight in his shaking hand. He hoped the light might spook the bear or coyote and cause it to run away. Randy rose to his feet and pointed the flashlight in the direction of the noise.

Then he laughed.

"What?" Bill said, coming out of the tent. "What is it?"

"It's the funniest-looking bear I ever did see," Randy said, shining his flashlight beam on a brown and white cow.

Bill laughed, too. "That's one of them cows from Hatcher's pasture. They get loose and wander off to the woods all the time. And you was so scared!"

"You was scared, too," Randy said, nudging Bill's shoulder.

"Was not." Bill patted the cow on the rump. "Get on home, Bessie!"

The cow ambled off in the general direction of the pasture.

"How did you know her name was Bessie?" Randy asked.

"I call all cows Bessie," Bill said. "They just look like Bessies to me."

Once the cow crisis was averted, they secured the tent and crawled back inside. Tired from all the excitement, Randy fell deeply asleep.

Randy was awakened by a low humming sound. It reminded him of a nest of wasps, but the sound was deeper, more musical somehow. Then, just as he was getting awake enough to try to make sense of things, the tent was illuminated with an eerie green glow.

Bill stirred and opened his eyes. "What the Sam Hill—?"

"I don't know," Randy said. This fear was different than when he thought there was a wild animal outside the tent. He had seen wild animals, had been taught what to do if faced with one. But he had no idea what could be producing that light and sound. It was a deeper fear, a fear that seemed to live deep in the pit of his stomach, the unsettling feeling of being afraid without having any idea what it was you were afraid of.

"Which is better, in the tent or out of the tent?" Bill asked, his voice trembling.

"I don't know that either," Randy said. He took a deep breath. "But I'd rather know what it is than not know. I'm going out there."

He held fast to the flashlight even though he didn't need it. The green glow was almost as bright as the light cast by an electric light bulb. The light grew brighter as he made his way out of the tent. His legs shook as he stood. The glow was so bright now that he had to shield his eyes. He turned, squinting, to look at where it glowed the brightest.

And then his mouth dropped open in shock.

"Randy, are you okay?" Bill was scrambling out of the tent. "What is it?"

Even if Randy could have found the words in his brain, he couldn't form them with his mouth. He could only mutely point.

The thing was floating, hovering just above them. It was big, larger than a big man, though whether it was male or female was not apparent. It appeared to be wearing a green hooded cloak over a green flowing robe, which rippled in the breeze. Its face was hard to see because of the hood, but its eyes were red and round, sending out beams like headlights. The green glow seemed to be emanating from its entire body, circling it like a halo.

Randy and Bill looked at one another as if to confirm they were really seeing what they thought they were seeing.

And then they screamed.

The thing, whatever it was, did not respond to them in any way, nor did it show any signs of moving closer.

Well, Randy wasn't going to give it the chance to decide to get closer. There was only one word he could reach in the terrified recesses of his brain, and he yelled it now: "Run!"

He ran across the clearing, abandoning their campsite. He heard Bill's rapid footfalls right behind him. But he wasn't going to look to see if the thing was chasing them. That's how people in movies always got in trouble. They looked back to see where the monster was, and then they lost their footing and fell, which gave the monster time to catch up with them.

The monster. That's what it was, wasn't it? He and Bill had seen a monster.

Running in the dark was hard, but Randy had his flashlight, and the remnants of the green glow kept the woods from being pitch-dark. All the same, Randy reached for Bill's hand so they could make their way over the roots and rocks together. At least this time they were going downhill.

When they reached the pasture that was between their houses, they wordlessly went their separate ways, Bill to his house, Randy to his. They were still running, though. Randy felt like his heart was going to thud right out of his chest.

The house was dark. He rushed to the front door and was relieved to find it unlocked. He swung open the door but froze when it creaked, and willed himself to slow down. He didn't want to wake anybody up because he didn't want to have to explain why he was home early from the camping trip or what he had seen. How could he explain it when he wasn't sure what it was himself?

Once inside, Randy tore off his shoes and carried them, tiptoeing to his room in his sock feet. Cindy was sleeping peacefully. He jumped into his bed, shoes in his arms and all, and pulled the covers over his head. *Deep breaths*, he told himself, but his breathing was shallow, like a scared rabbit's, and he couldn't stop shaking. *You're safe*, he told himself. *It didn't follow you. You're safe.*

Just to make sure, he poked his head out of the covers and peeked out the window, half expecting to see the weird, glowing face looking right at him. But it wasn't there. Everything outside seemed ordinary until Randy moved his gaze out toward the mountains. He was pretty sure there was a faint green glow coming up from the trees.

CHAPTER 3

Randy's family always tried to have a big noon dinner on Sunday, but it had gotten harder since Daddy lost his job. Back when the mining money was good, Sunday dinner would be two kinds of meat and all kinds of vegetables—corn on the cob, tomatoes and cucumbers, cabbage, fried okra—plus biscuits and corn bread. Today the meal was less lavish, country ham biscuits and some green beans Momma had canned last summer.

It was good food, but Randy didn't have much of an appetite. He was too panicked and puzzled by what he'd seen the night before. He was desperate to talk to Bill, but he knew there was no use trying to talk to Bill on a Sunday. For Bill's family, church was an all-day affair. There was Sunday school, then church services followed by a big picnic, then singing until it was time for the evening services. Momma made Randy and his sister go to church a couple times a month, but they were nowhere near as devout as Bill's family.

"Hey, I've eat more ham biscuits than Randy," Cindy said, gesturing toward her brother with a biscuit in hand. "I've had three and he ain't had but one."

"Randy, are you feeling all right?" Momma asked. "You didn't catch a chill out in the woods last night, did you?"

"No, ma'am, I'm not sick," Randy said. He wasn't eating was because what he saw the night before was tearing him up inside. He needed to talk about it, needed to unburden himself of the secret. He was a pretty quiet kid, but when something bad happened, the only way he could feel better was to talk about it. *Okay*, he told himself. *Out with it.* "Something happened last night that . . . troubled me," he said.

"Did you and Bill get in a fight?" Cindy asked, grinning around a mouthful of ham biscuit. She seemed pretty entertained by the prospect.

"No, nothing like that," Randy said. "I guess you could say we saw something."

"Did you come across somebody's still?" Daddy asked, spearing a forkful of green beans. It was common knowledge that there were lots of moonshiners who set up their illegal whiskey making contraptions in the hills. They didn't take kindly to strangers who discovered their whereabouts.

"No, nothing like that neither," Randy said, pushing his plate away. How could he explain something that seemed so unexplainable? What were the chances that anybody would even believe him? But Momma always said, "The truth will set you free." If he was going to deal with what had happened, he had to tell the truth. He took a deep breath, then willed himself to speak. "We was asleep in the tent, and this strange light woke me up. It was green like some of the lights they put up downtown at Christmastime, except it gave off more of a glow. It woke Bill up, too, and we went outside to see what it was." He paused. Momma and Daddy and Cindy were all staring at him like he was a stranger who had sat down at the table with them, but he had to keep talking. He had to finish the story. "And to tell the truth, I can't tell you what it was. It was shaped kind of like a person but bigger, and you couldn't see its shape or its face real good because it had on this cape with a big hood. But its eyes were big and round and glowed red." He looked again at his parents' and sister's faces. They were all wearing looks of shock and confusion. Cindy looked like she was trying to figure out if he was joking or not.

Finally, Momma gave a nervous little laugh. "Well, I reckon you boys got to telling spooky stories out there in the dark woods and got yourselves all worked up. You probably just seen a big hoot owl or something."

"Yeah," Daddy said, "sometimes critters you wouldn't think nothing of in the daytime look downright frightful at night. One time when I was taking out the trash in the evening, a possum sprung out at me and scared the living daylights out of me. It was baring its teeth and hissing, and its eyes glowed just like you was saying."

But owls and possums were nothing like what Randy had been describing. "No, it wasn't like that," Randy said. "It was big and green and floating and it gave off this light—"

"Sometimes our minds can play tricks on us," Momma said. "Especially when you're out at night with your friend and you've stayed up way past your bedtime trying to scare each other. I bet y'all hardly got a wink of sleep last night. Maybe you should lie down for a nap once you're done eating."

"I am done, Mama. Can I be excused?"

Randy didn't want to nap, but he saw it was pointless to continue the conversation. The more he insisted that he knew what he had seen, the more likely his family was to think he was crazy. He lay across his bed with a composition book and a pencil. He closed his eyes for a moment, picturing the monster, then he started to draw. He wasn't a great artist, but by the time he was done, he had a reasonably good likeness of what he had seen. It made him feel a little better to have the image, even though he didn't need to look at a picture to remember what the monster looked like. How could you see something like that and ever forget it?

And if someone had never seen a monster, you couldn't possibly make them understand what it was like. The only person who could understand was someone who had had the experience, too. First thing tomorrow, he needed to talk to Bill.

Randy woke up Monday morning feeling hopeful. Once he talked to Bill, things would be clearer, and he would feel less alone.

"You feeling better now that you've had a chance to rest?" Momma asked as she set his breakfast of biscuits and gravy in front of him.

"Yes, ma'am," Randy said, though of course he hadn't felt bad in quite the way Momma meant.

"Sometimes you just need to see things clearer in the light of a new day," Daddy said. He was drinking coffee and looking at the newspaper's want ads. He had a pencil ready to circle any possible jobs, but he hadn't circled anything yet.

Randy glanced at the cuckoo clock above the icebox. Bill was never late but apparently there was a first time for everything. An image of Bill huddled under the covers flashed in Randy's mind and he regretted not trying harder to check on his friend yesterday. What if Bill was still curled up in bed, shaking from what they had seen?

There was a loud banging on the screen door and Randy jumped. Bill let himself in.

"Hi, Bill!" Cindy said, her whole face lighting up.

"Hey, Cindy," Bill said. He had his school satchel slung over his shoulder and was wearing slightly nicer clothes than the ones he wore just to play in.

So not still shaking in bed. *Good*, Randy thought.

"You got time for a biscuit this morning?" Momma asked.

"Not to set down and eat one, but I'll take one for the road," Bill said, grinning.

"Yeah, we'd better get going," Randy said, getting up from the table. He wasn't particularly anxious to get to school, but he was dying to get Bill alone so they could talk.

Momma handed Bill a warm biscuit wrapped in a

napkin, and he bit into it immediately. "Thank you, Miz Siler. Your biscuits is better than my momma's, but don't tell my momma I said that."

Momma smiled. "I wouldn't dream of it."

Randy grabbed his books and the boys headed out. They always walked together to the head of the hollow to catch the school bus. Randy figured the ten-minute walk would be a good opportunity for them to talk about what they had seen on Saturday night.

Once they were on the gravel road that led out to the main road, Randy said, "You know, I've been thinking a lot about that thing we saw."

"Me too," Bill said, "and I think I've got it all figured out."

"Figured out how?" Randy asked. If Bill had any ideas, Randy certainly wanted to hear them.

"Well, I had it figured out as soon as I seen it, really," Bill said. "It was a hoax. Like 'The War of the Worlds.'"

A hoax? The knot in Randy's stomach sure didn't think it was a hoax, but he also didn't know what Bill was talking about. "What's 'The War of the Worlds'?"

"It was a radio show that came on when my daddy was a little boy," Bill said. "It sounded like a news broadcast and was all about how the Martians had come to earth and was about to take over. Daddy said it had his Pa so convinced that he was loading his rifle, ready to fight off the Martians."

"So you think the thing we saw wasn't real?" The thought hadn't even crossed Randy's mind.

Bill laughed. "Oh, I knew right away it wasn't real! Here's what I think. It was the Russians who put out the hoax."

Randy stifled the urge to roll his eyes. "Why would the Russians try to trick us thataway?" Randy asked. "Especially you and me. We're just kids. We're not important to them."

"I'm sure we're not the only people it appeared to," Bill said. "If the Russians scare enough people with that thing and make everyone think we're under attack, then everybody would be so scared of aliens that they won't notice the Russians taking over the country."

Randy shook his head. "It looked real." He could see the round, glowing eyes just as surely as if they were staring at him right now.

"Sure it did. I'm sure the Reds got some of their best people working on it to make sure it looks real."

Randy didn't have an explanation himself for the incident, but Bill's explanation felt awfully far-fetched. "So you say you knew it was fake when you saw it?"

"I sure did." Bill's shoulders were slung back. He looked pleased with himself.

"Then why was you so scared?"

Bill's eyes flashed mad. "I wasn't scared. *You* was the one that was scared."

Randy laughed. He remembered the look on Bill's face, the wide eyes, the slack jaw. "We was both scared. We screamed, then we ran like scalded dogs."

"Yeah, well," Bill said as they approached the bus stop. "I was just pretending to be scared to throw the Russians off track. You're the one who was the big chicken."

As much as Randy liked the chickens at the farm, he didn't want to be one. "Come on, Bill, we both had our britches scared off. Either both of us is chickens, or neither one of us is!"

Bill tucked his hands into his armpits and flapped his arms like wings. "Bock, bock, bock!" He danced around Randy.

Before Randy could think of a comeback, the bus arrived. He climbed on first and took his customary seat on the third row by the window. For the first time he could remember, Bill didn't come sit beside him.

ABOUT THE AUTHOR

Elley Cooper writes fiction for young adults and adults. She has always loved horror and is grateful whenever she can spend time in a dark and twisted universe. Elley lives in Tennessee with her family and many spoiled pets and can often be found writing books with Kevin Anderson & Associates.